"Let Me Know If There's Anything Else I Can Do For You, Sheriff . . ."

Amanda said.

Vince stared at her with a penetrating look that peeled away the layers of indifference she'd tried to build against him.

"You know what you can do for me," he whispered.

A chill ran down her back at the raspy promise in his voice, and she closed her eyes to break the contact.

"You never give up, do you? I hope you're this diligent in your work," she said.

Vince laughed and squinted his eyes, "Never fear, Mrs. Simpson, I always get my man." He leaned over the desk and brought his face within inches of hers. "And my woman."

Dear Reader:

Welcome to the world of Silhouette Desire. Join me as we travel to a land of incredible passion and tantalizing romance—a place where dreams can, and do, come true.

When I read a Silhouette Desire, I sometimes feel as if I'm going on a little vacation. I can relax, put my feet up and become transported to a new world... a world that has, naturally, a perfect hero just waiting to whisk me away! These are stories to remember, containing moments to treasure.

Silhouette Desire novels are romantic love stories—sensuous yet emotional. As a reader, you not only see the hero and heroine fall in love, you also feel what they're feeling.

In upcoming books look for some of your favorite Silhouette Desire authors: Joan Hohl, BJ James, Linda Lael Miller and Diana Palmer.

So enjoy!

Lucia Macro
Senior Editor

AUDRA ADAMS

PEOPLE WILL TALK

SILHOUETTE *Desire*

Published by Silhouette Books New York

America's Publisher of Contemporary Romance

SILHOUETTE BOOKS
300 East 42nd St., New York, N.Y. 10017

ISBN: 0-373-05592-7

First Silhouette Books printing September 1990

Printed in the U.S.A.

AUDRA ADAMS

has always been in love with love and believed in happy endings. What better reason to become a romance writer? She has stored away a wellspring of inspiration from her first readings of *Cinderella* right up to meeting her husband, who proposed eight days after they met. "They" said it wouldn't last, but eleven years and two children later, the marriage is still going strong.

A transplanted New York City woman who has fallen under the spell of the Jersey shore, Audra Adams dreams up new characters and stories as she stares out at the rolling ocean waves. She's an incurable optimist who feels that life should be lived to the fullest, and if it is, romance will find you.

To my critique group:
Helen Cavanagh, Donna Fletcher, Kaye Gilmartin,
Suzanne Hoos and Johnnie Ryan-Evans . . .
the best of the best.

One

Hi, Mom! Hi, Uncle John! What's for dinner?''

Nine-and-a-half-year-old Sean Scott Simpson bounded into the kitchen and almost knocked over his mother with his overbearing but loving hug. Like an overgrown puppy, his hands and feet were too big for his body, and yet he was still growing like a weed. It was obvious to Amanda that he took after his football-playing father. At times he even displayed his sire's brazen, outgoing personality. Fortunately, she thought, it was much cuter at almost-ten then it had been at thirty.

"Hi, Sean. Have a good time at Cory's?"

"Yeah," he said, grabbing a celery stalk and stuffing it into his mouth. "We played video games most of the time. It was too cold to ride bikes."

"Don't talk with your mouth full," Amanda admonished as she stopped the boy from helping himself to another stalk. "Dinner's almost ready. Go wash your hands then set the table in the dining room."

"We having company or something?"

"What am I, chopped liver?" John teased.

"Nah!" Sean laughed as his uncle ruffled his hair. "It's just you're always here! Who else is coming?"

"Aunt Polly will be here soon," Amanda said. "Now move it. I'm running late."

"As usual," her son said with a grin on his freckled face. Amanda returned a mock menacing look as he left the room.

John smiled and walked toward the sink. "He's a great kid, Amanda."

"Thanks. I know." She smiled broadly. "He and Kim keep me going."

"You should get out more. It can't be much fun spending Saturday night with Polly and me."

Amanda opened the refrigerator and took out a cellophane-wrapped head of lettuce. She nudged her younger brother away from the sink as she split it down the middle and held it under the tap.

"I'm perfectly happy spending my weekends with the family. I work all week. It's my only time to be with the kids."

"Polly's cousin Pete is coming to town next week."

"Don't start, John. I've told you and Polly a thousand times. I'm not interested."

"You remember Pete, don't you? You met him at our wedding."

"John! That was ten years ago. I was married to Bill and pregnant with Sean. I wasn't exactly looking at men at the time."

"And you're still not. Bill did a real job on you, didn't he?" John said. "My God, Amanda, it's been five years since you split. How long are you going to carry a torch for the guy?''

Amanda turned her back to him and faced the sink. She picked up the vegetable brush and vigorously scrubbed a huge Idaho potato. She barely listened as her brother rehashed the same old story of her life. Little did he, or anyone for that matter, know the *relief* she'd felt the day Bill walked into the California sunset with his new honey. That little twenty-two-year-old airline stewardess had been a most welcome blessing in disguise.

Billy Simpson was a high school jock who never grew up. From a neighboring city, he was everything the hometown boys were not—stylish, confident and definitely interested in the shy, overprotected seventeen-year-old Amanda. He pursued her that summer with a single-mindedness she'd later come to know as only an immature stubborn streak. But at that time in her life, he represented the fun and freedom she had never known. Dating Billy against her parents' wishes was her one rebellious act, and it certainly changed her life. But she fell in love that summer, and she wanted him. *Be careful of what you wish for...*

"Why won't you at least meet Pete? He's a great guy. And anyway, he'll only be in town a few weeks."

Amanda's head snapped around, her dark brown eyes challenging.

"If he's only going to be here for a few weeks, why should I bother? What if I like him? Or he likes me? You and Polly are always telling me to get married again." She smugly placed the wet potato on the drain board and picked up another. "Poor Petey and I are doomed from the start."

"You could move away from Branchport, you know."

"Never again."

Branchport, for all its faults, was her home, not to mention a great place to raise her children. In his eternal pursuit for happiness and a quick road to riches, Billy had moved his young family hither and yon. The job was never good enough, the boss always unreasonable, the city or town too small for his big plans. When the marriage ended, Amanda returned to her hometown, the one place that represented stability in her life. She had no intentions of ever leaving it again.

"What's this town ever done for you except gossip about you?"

Amanda slammed the second cleaned potato down and turned. Enough was enough.

"Why are you here, John?"

John Hatcher straightened his frame away from the island counter. "You invited me to dinner."

"Yes. But why are you here so early?"

"I came to help."

Rifling through a cabinet, Amanda found a large monkeypod salad bowl. She placed the two lettuce halves into it and put the wood bowl down in front of John.

"Then stop lecturing and help. Make the salad."

John shook his head as he began shredding the lettuce into the bowl. "You can't run away forever, Amanda. One of these days when you least expect it, some guy's going to come along and—"

The doorbell rang.

"Who could that be?" Amanda asked as she wiped her wet hands on a dish towel. No one rang her bell. The door was always open, and the kids, Polly, her neighbors, *everyone* always just walked right in. That's the way it was in Branchport....

Throwing the dish towel over her shoulder, Amanda opened the front door. A blast of frigid January wind assaulted her as she found herself face-to-face with a shiny tin star, the word *SHERIFF* emblazoned across its width. It took her a moment to realize there was a rather large man attached to it. Her eyes slowly traveled from the badge to the stern, serious face of its owner.

"Are you Mrs. Simpson?"

"Yes...?"

It was then she recognized the small figure cowering behind the officer.

"Kimberly! Good Lord! What is this all about?" She pulled the girl to her, placing herself between the lawman and her child.

"Oh, Mom—"

"Your daughter, ma'am, was picked up at the mall with a boy by the name of—" he checked a piece of paper in his hand "—Thomas Bronson, age sixteen." He looked back at her. "He was picked up for shoplifting."

"Kimberly? What happened? Were you—"

"I was with Tommy and some of his friends. We weren't doing anything wrong!" she shouted, and then ran up the stairs to her room, slamming the door.

Amanda turned back to the sheriff. She was frozen to the spot, whether from the icy wind or the steel-gray eyes, she wasn't entirely sure.

"Please, come in, Sheriff...?"

He stepped inside and shut the door behind him.

"Messina. Vincent Messina."

She knew who he was now. He'd just started as Branchport's new sheriff, temporarily replacing the ailing Odus Tucker, who'd been a town fixture for more than three decades. Messina was a former New York City cop. She'd read about it in the local paper.

The picture that accompanied the story hadn't done him justice, she decided. He was handsome, dark, with a brooding quality about him, not at all as sinister as the black-and-white, grainy photo had suggested. His face was strong, features defined—high wide cheekbones, a slightly crooked Roman nose, and a squared jaw. His eyes were riveting, large, deep-set and slate-gray.

And then there was his full bottom lip...

Amanda mentally shook herself. This was neither the time nor the place to critique his lips, upper or lower. She tore her gaze away and returned to the business at hand.

"What exactly happened, Sheriff Messina?" she asked, removing the dish towel from her shoulder.

Vince didn't answer immediately. He was studying the woman before him with the same intensity he'd recognized in her perusal of him. She was petite, with short, light brown curls and eyes the color of bittersweet chocolate. She looked too young by far to be the mother of a teenager, but the hand on her hip and that look in her eye more than told him she was, indeed, and that she was as fiercely defensive as any mother bear protecting her cub.

Amanda lifted herself to her full meager height as she awaited his explanation. He was taking her measure, and for some strange reason that had nothing to do with Kimberly and her problem, she didn't want to come up short in the evaluation.

"Your daughter and some of her friends were at the mall today. From what I've been told by the store manager, she and this Thomas Bronson were together when he stole a pair of sunglasses off a rack. She seemed a little young to be mixed up with this sort of thing, so I brought her home."

"I find it hard to believe that she or Tommy were stealing anything. There must be some mistake. They're good kids!"

"Even 'good kids' get in trouble, Mrs. Simpson. I've seen it happen enough times. Kids do their own thing, and the parents aren't even aware of what's going on."

Amanda became indignant. Was he implying that she didn't know what her teenager was doing?

"Perhaps that's the way it is in New York, Sheriff Messina, but in Branchport we know where our children are."

"I'm not suggesting that you don't—"

"What's the problem?" John interrupted as he walked into the room.

"The sheriff brought Kimberly home from the mall. He says Tommy was shoplifting."

"That's ridiculous!" John said. "There must be some mistake."

Vince eyed the man who came up behind Amanda. A short, sharp, fleeting wave of disappointment stabbed at him, then was gone.

"No mistake, Mr. Simpson," Vince said. "Your daughter shouldn't be associating with these older boys."

"I'm not Mr. Simpson," John said, extending his hand toward Vince. "John Hatcher. I own the hardware store in town."

Vince shook hands and revised his initial assumption. Not husband, he said to himself as he watched John stand beside Amanda—lover. He took a backward step toward the door.

"Can we get back to the point?" Amanda said.

"Of course," Vince said. "I brought the boy down to the station, and the deputy is contacting his parents. As I said before, I thought it best to bring Kimberly home myself and speak to you personally. She's . . . how old?"

"Fourteen."

"Yes." He checked his sheet again. "Although she wasn't charged with anything, she needs a good talking-to before things get out of hand."

"I'll handle it," she answered curtly. Amanda's chin jutted outward. "Now if you'll excuse me, I need to talk to my daughter."

Not waiting to see the sheriff's reaction to her rudeness, Amanda ran up the stairs and stood outside her daughter's room. She bit her bottom lip and closed her eyes for a moment to clear her head of all thoughts, save one. Kimberly needed her.

"Honey?" She knocked. "Can I come in?"

She heard a low "Sure" and opened the door to find Kim lying diagonally across the bed on her stomach, her head cradled in her arms.

Amanda approached slowly and sat down next to the sprawled girl. She rubbed her hand across her daughter's back, the heavy cable-knit sweater feeling coarse and lumpy to the touch.

"Want to tell me what happened?"

Kim rolled over and faced her. "We didn't do anything wrong, Mom. Honest."

"I know. Just tell me."

Kim sighed. "Tommy and me were in Mc-
Donough's Five-and-Ten, just looking. We were fool-
ing around a little, you know? Anyway, he tried on a
pair of sunglasses and we laughed. He pushed them on
top of his head and tried on some more. When we left
the store, after checking out the tapes, he forgot he had
the first pair of sunglasses on his head. The guard
stopped us at the door. He didn't want to hear it! He
started yelling at us and called the manager. The manager called the police."

"Didn't you explain this to the sheriff?"

"Yes! A hundred times! It didn't matter. He took
Tommy to the police station, and then said he was taking me home. Peggy Widman actually *saw* me in the
police car! I was mortified! Oh, Mom, I can't go to
school Monday, I just can't!"

Kimberly covered her face with her hands and
sobbed.

Amanda ran her fingers through the long chestnut
hair soothingly.

"Don't worry about school. We'll think of something. I'm sure after the police talk to Tommy's parents, this will all be straightened out."

"Why did he have to drive me home?" Kim
groaned.

"I know. It was thoughtless. He's from New York.
It will take him awhile to get used to things around
here. I suppose he doesn't really understand how people are affected by that sort of thing here." Amanda
stroked her daughter's head again. "Everything will be
all right, you'll see. We'll work it out together."

Kimberly turned her face away and hugged the pillow, and Amanda's heart went out to her. Nobody

knew better than she how humiliating it was to be the main topic of gossip in town.

Amanda stood and looked around the room. A photograph in a wooden frame sat on her dresser. She lifted it and stared at the images. Kim was about three, sitting on Bill's lap, with Amanda, visibly pregnant with Sean, standing nearby. They seemed like such an ordinary, happy family. She supposed that was why Kim kept the photo. There were too few memories of happy times during that marriage.

She replaced the frame and shook her head. There were many things she'd come to dislike about her life with Bill, but the two children he gave her were a combination of the best of both of them, and she'd never regretted having them for a minute.

But was the sheriff right? Kim was a teenager now, with Sean close on her trail. Could she handle two teenagers all by herself? She'd never given it much thought until this incident happened. What had he said? Something about not knowing what was going on. Was she too busy with her job, the house and worrying about making ends meet, that she was missing those small, daily signals sent out by her children?

"We'll talk again later. I'll call you when dinner's ready," Amanda said softly before leaving.

"I'm not hungry," came the muffled response.

Amanda shut the door as she left, thinking it best to leave Kim alone for now. Sean was waiting for her on the stairway.

"What happened, Mommy?"

Amanda put her arm around her son. He always reverted to "Mommy" after a nightmare or when he was hurt, scared.

"Kim had a little problem at the mall today. I'll tell you about it after dinner, okay?"

"Can I see her?"

"Not right now. She wants to be alone for a while. Why don't you play video games until dinnertime?"

"Okay," he said, easily reassured. "Cory let me borrow his new game from Christmas. I still can't get to the princess."

She kissed his cheek. "Keep trying, you'll do it."

As he thumped to his room, Amanda descended the stairs and returned to the kitchen to finish making dinner. She was taken back for a moment to find John and the sheriff sitting at the table, and a fresh pot of coffee on the stove.

Vince stood as she entered the room. He could tell she was surprised to see him still here. She covered it well, he thought as she walked past him and poured herself a cup of coffee.

He had no idea why he *was* still here. He was on duty, had to work most of the weekend and certainly didn't have the time for idle chitchat.

But when the petite Mrs. Simpson had opened the front door, he'd felt as if he'd been sucker-punched. A shiver had rocked his body that had nothing to do with the below-freezing temperature. That a woman should affect him so on sight was unusual in itself; that a woman in this backwater town should, was incredible.

"Was there something else, Sheriff?" she asked, her back to him as she poured milk into her mug.

Vince smiled to himself. Cool as a cucumber, he thought, when all she wants to do is chew my head off.

"No, not on my end. I thought you might have something you'd want me to do."

"No," she said calmly as she slowly turned to face him. "I think you've done enough for one day, don't you?"

"Now," John interjected. "There's no need to be rude. The sheriff was nice enough to bring Kim home—"

"Home in a squad car! My daughter's not a criminal, for pete's sake! She hasn't even been charged with anything. What will people think seeing her paraded through town by the police? I think, Sheriff, you may have overreacted. Perhaps a bit too zealous your first week on the job?" She smiled sweetly, daggers in her big brown eyes.

The daggers were returned, piercing, steel-gray shards of light aimed directly at her. She didn't care. All her bottled anger uncapped and spewed forth. Who did he think he was dragging Kimberly home? An idiot would know that people thrived on this sort of gossip. She had no desire to see her daughter subjected to what she went through long ago....

Vince picked up his hat from the table. "I did what I thought best—"

"I would have preferred it if you had called me and asked what I thought."

They stared at each other in silent combat for a long moment.

"I'll keep that in mind next time," he said softly as he made his way to the front door.

"There won't be a next time, Sheriff."

Vince turned as John came up behind Amanda and placed his hands on her shoulders. Amanda knew he misinterpreted their relationship as his gaze passed from her to John and back again. She felt her face turn crimson, and had to stop herself from correcting him. Let him think what he wanted; she couldn't care less.

The sheriff opened the door and turned. "For your sake, I hope you're right. I'd keep her away from that boy."

"Or what?"

"Or next time it may not be so simple as a ride home in a squad car."

"Is that a threat, Sheriff?"

"No, ma'am. A warning." He returned the hat to his head and tugged on the rim. The obvious courtesy irked her to no end. She slammed the door at his back.

"Well, of all the nerve—"

"That was uncalled for, Amanda," John said. "The man was only doing his job, and doing it quite well, too. He could have made you come down to the station to pick her up. It was nice of him—"

"Nice? Nice! For heaven's sake, John, *think*! Old Hester Waterbury across the street has had her nose cemented to the window since he arrived! Now everyone will know what happened!"

"You care too much about people. It's no one's business."

"That's easy for you to say. You don't have to put up with the gossips. And poor Kimberly!"

John came up and put his arms around her. "Come on. Calm down," he said. "Give it time. It'll blow over. It always does."

Amanda shut her eyes and hugged her brother tightly, eager for the comfort he gave.

"Very wise words, John, and very true. But then, who knows that better than me?"

Vince Messina shut the refrigerator door. It was nearly empty, and the little that was inside was unappetizing. He wasn't hungry, anyway. Just tired. He'd worked double shifts all weekend, out of choice not necessity, and now he was paying for it. He rubbed a hand over his day-old beard and scratched his chin as he glanced at the clock on the wall. Ten after midnight.

After a quick shower he fell into bed, yet sleep was elusive. The flipping numbers of his clock radio echoed through the small bedroom of his rented cottage. There were no other sounds from within or without. The frigid January weather obliterated all life on the frozen lake that the house abutted. A blast of steam heat rattled the baseboard radiators then clattered to a low hiss.

All was calm. Everywhere, that is, except inside Vince's head.

Why wouldn't it go away? Why couldn't he forget? It'd been over a year already, closer to two, and still, whenever there was a quiet moment, thoughts of that night sprang to life. He could still see his partner, Ed Lewis, fall beside him, could still feel the cold metal of the gun in his hand as he instinctively fired at the assailant. That his friend's murderer was only fifteen didn't come out until later. Everyone told him it didn't matter; the kid was a criminal, a cop killer.

But it did matter to Vince. He'd used the gun before. It was part of his job. But never directed toward a kid. The guilt had almost driven him mad, especially after the boy's mother had asked to see him. He never did go. He couldn't deal with her accusations and tears. Forget it, they told him—his fellow cops, his father and uncle, former cops themselves. Let it go. The boy was a thief and he would have killed you as sure as he did Ed. It was the right thing to do. The only thing.

Yet he couldn't come to terms with it. When his twenty years were up, he planned to collect his pension and quit. He knew he was a ripe candidate for therapy, but he'd been raised to work things out himself, without help from anyone. So, on the advice of his captain, he'd taken a six-month leave of absence to get his head together. A change of scenery and time to forget were the best medicine.

When his Uncle Louis had called him with this job offer, it had seemed like a godsend. Odus Tucker, the sheriff of Branchport, had suffered a heart attack and had to take it easy for a while. Odus and Lou had worked together on a kidnapping case back in the fifties and had been fast friends ever since. Take over until he's up and around again, his uncle had urged. Louis knew the small town in upstate New York well. A good fishing town, he had joked. Do an old friend a favor, and help yourself at the same time. Branchport was a perfect place to mend.

Vince took a deep breath. So here he was for two, maybe three months at best. But he was restless. As picturesque as the town was, it wasn't home. Vince Messina was a city boy, Bronx born and bred. He had worked in some of the toughest neighborhoods in New York for almost twenty years, signing on as one of New York's Finest right out of high school. It had been a good life, and until the incident with Ed and the boy, he'd never had any regrets.

Staring at the crack that ran the length of the ceiling, Vince threw his arm across his forehead. Maybe Linda. That was a regret. They had been divorced five years already. The marriage fell apart soon after he was shot. It was only a flesh wound, but Linda went crazy every time he left the house after that. A year later she was gone, taking their little girl with her to Florida. She'd remarried and was raising his daughter with her new husband. He saw Chrissy as often as he could, and she came north to spend his vacation with him, but it wasn't the same. She was fourteen already...same age as that kid today. What was her name? Kimberly Simpson.

And her mother. There was something about that woman....

He rolled onto his side. He was no saint, and was by no means shy with women, but nothing of interest had come his way in a long time. Until this one.

I wonder what her first name is?

He'd find out. If he'd learned anything in the short time he'd been in Branchport, it was that everyone knew everything about everybody in this town. In many ways that bothered him, but now he was kind of glad. If he'd met her in New York, chances were he'd never see her again in his entire life. But here, in Branchport...well, that was another case entirely. These people were nosy as hell, but he had to admit, they were also kind. The ladies in town were forever sending over casseroles and pies, and the men went out of their way to make him feel a part of the community. It was all very new to him. He had an innate distrust of strangers, learning early that street smarts were more important than popularity. But everyone he met here seemed to go out of their way to welcome him— everyone that is, except the feisty Mrs. Simpson.

I wonder what her story is?

She seemed pretty chummy with that John Hatcher. If she was involved with him, so be it. No problem. He didn't even know her. Hell, come to think of it, he didn't even like her!

Vince felt the fingers of sleep descend and offered himself to be sacrificed. The last thing his mind registered was a small, gamine face with large brown eyes framed with soft, brown curls.

Two

Amanda stared at the stack of manila folders on her desk. No matter what she did, she couldn't seem to concentrate. It was midday already, and she'd yet to take a lunch break.

After the disastrous weekend, she hadn't been able to get her mind back to business. Glancing at her wristwatch, she groaned. Almost two o'clock and she still hadn't finished opening the day's mail.

She wondered how Kimberly was faring. Her daughter had refused to take the school bus this morning, and Amanda had driven her. They'd talked about what happened for the umpteenth time, and Amanda had voiced her concerns about Tommy. Kim had quickly come to the boy's defense, but Amanda had been firm. Until she found out what his problem was, she didn't want Kim associating with him.

"I'll be leaving for the day, Amanda. Any urgent calls, you can find me with Statler over at the bank."

Amanda looked up to see her boss, Mike Powell, newly elected mayor of Branchport. As with most of the people in town her age, they'd gone to school together and had known each other since kindergarten. She liked Mike and was happy when he'd won the election. He was smart and not at all chauvinistic as the last mayor had been. He'd admired her initiative and had recently promoted her to administrative assistant. A hard worker, he only used the "good ole boy" network in town when it was to his advantage. Mike was going places, and if she played her cards right, she'd go right along with him.

"Okay. I'll answer any correspondence I can on my own and leave the rest for you for the morning."

"Fine," Mike said on his way out the door. "And if you have time, check my desk. It's a mess, as usual."

"Go!" she said with the wave of her hand. Mike was bright, and a good politician, but he was a disaster when it came to paperwork.

Amanda picked up a small paper bag from under her desk and unwrapped a turkey sandwich that she began to munch as she sorted through the mail. It wasn't much, but it would keep her stomach from growling. She needed to run to Polly's salon for a haircut after work and knew she'd be starving by the dinner hour if she didn't eat now. She made a fresh pot of coffee and took a ten-minute break before tackling Mike's office.

He was right; it was a mess. She sat behind his desk in the oversize, leather, swivel chair and made stacks of the folders and papers that were strewn across its surface. A red-tagged file caught her eye. A second glance confirmed what she'd thought she'd seen as she pulled the file folder out from the stack and laid it on the desk in front of her. The name "Vincent Messina" called out to her. She lifted her right hand and brought it slowly to rest on top of the folder, debating with herself whether or not to peruse its contents.

Of course she was curious; she wouldn't be human if she wasn't. She tapped her neatly manicured nails rhythmically as she attempted to convince herself that she really wasn't interested. He had nothing to do with her; his life was none of her business.

Just a peek, she thought, and opened the folder. A neatly typed résumé lay open to her view. A small ID photo adorned the top right-hand corner of the sheet of paper. It was the same photo that appeared in the local paper announcing his arrival.

She picked up the sheet and stared intently at the picture. His expression was glum, severe. She supposed that was the way policemen posed, hoping for a look that instilled respect and fear. But her memory of his face was crystal-clear, and this looked nothing like him. His hair was thicker and darker, almost black, and his brows dipped into a slight frown as they canopied his deep-set slate eyes. The nose looked the same, slightly crooked, as if it had been broken long ago and never properly healed.

But it was his mouth that held a fascination for her like no other. His lips were full, particularly his bottom lip, which seemed to protrude just enough to tempt her to rub her mouth against it, lick it, bite it, draw it into her mouth and . . .

She dropped the paper as if it were on fire. Stop it! she told herself. Lifting her hands, she pressed her cold palms to her flushed face. Her heart began to palpitate from a long-forgotten feeling that was as familiar as it was forbidden. She'd been without a man for a long time; some said too long. But it suited her fine. She liked her life the way it was, and no stranger was going to walk in and mess it up.

More objectively, she read through the résumé. He'd been a cop for close to twenty years, received several citations for bravery, and a commendation from the mayor when he was wounded in the line of duty some years ago. For a moment a frown crossed her brow as she wondered how seriously he'd been injured and if it was the reason for that brooding look of his.

She discovered he'd been married, had a child, a daughter, and divorced. From her date of birth, Amanda calculated that his daughter and Kim were about the same age. Did that explain the protective interest he took in Kim? Did he see his own daughter in her and want to help? The sobering thought changed her perspective of the situation at the mall dramatically. Perhaps she'd misjudged him....

"Hello?"

Amanda looked up and opened her mouth to reply, but no sound emerged. Vince Messina stood in the office doorway, leaning against the doorjamb. She blinked in an attempt to ascertain if he was real or an image her guilty conscience had conjured up.

He wore a light blue shirt with gray vertical stripes that was unbuttoned just enough at the collar to show a few tufts of dark curly chest hair. The bleached jeans were tightly molded onto his muscled legs and sexy as hell.

"Hello." She found her voice.

Vince pushed himself away from the door and took a step into the office. "Something wrong?" he asked.

"No, nothing's wrong. Nothing at all. It's just that I almost didn't recognize you out of uniform."

"I'm off today," he said. "Did double duty this weekend."

Amanda quickly snapped the folder shut in front of her. She picked up several other files and placed them on top of his, shuffling them and looking as efficient as she possibly could.

"What can I do for you?"

"I'm looking for the mayor's office."

"You've found it."

Vince's eyebrows lifted in surprise. "You work here?"

"Yes, I'm Mike Powell's administrative assistant."

Vince took a moment to study her face, that same face that had invaded his dreams. He hadn't expected to see her this soon, but here she was, dressed in a white blouse and dove-gray suit, acting very professional as she sat in a chair that looked big enough to swallow her.

He stood stock-still and stared. Their gazes locked and held for a breath of a moment. There it was again, that zing, that fist in his gut. The same feeling he'd had the first time he'd seen her.

He cleared his throat. "Then I guess you're the one to see."

"Please," Amanda said. Her voice sounded breathy. "Have a seat."

He sat across from her and crossed his leg at a right angle. Leaning forward, he reached into his back pocket and extracted an envelope and handed it to her.

"Odus Tucker told me to check with the mayor's office on tax and insurance forms to be filled out."

"Oh, yes," she said. "But I don't have those forms in here. This is Mike's office. Give me a minute and I'll get them for you."

She almost ran from the room, fleeing more from those unsettling eyes than from her guilt at being caught. Opening the file cabinet near her desk, she found the packet of forms he requested. As she slammed the metal drawer and turned, she bumped right into him.

They stood toe-to-toe, Amanda's face staring into the soft cotton fabric of his shirt. She took a deep breath to calm herself, but his scent filled her nostrils and her stomach flip-flopped. Slowly she looked up at his face.

She wasn't so far gone that she didn't recognize desire when she saw it. It was plainly etched on his taut features. An answering tug reverberated inside her and she took a step back in fear of it. Her back hit the file cabinet, and the cold metal jolted her to her senses.

"Here." She held out the packet of forms. "You can take them with you and return them to me at your leisure."

Vince accepted the papers. He sensed her discomfort with his nearness and stepped away. His reaction to this woman was insane, and he knew it; but for the life of him, he couldn't curtail it.

He never lost control. It was part of his job training, and he was a master at it. The thought that this tiny woman could undo years of discipline was unfathomable. He summoned to mind a cold shower in an attempt to lower his pulse rate and diminish his ardor. Mrs. Simpson, he knew instinctively, was not the type of woman to go in for a one-night stand. And the way his life was right now, he couldn't offer much more than that.

"I'd like to fill them out now, if you don't mind?" He'd just as well get it done with. Then, maybe, he wouldn't run into her again; that in itself might solve the problem.

"No," she said, avoiding his eyes. "Go right ahead." She cleared a spot on the corner of her desk for him to work, then returned to Mike's office.

Out of his view, she gripped the arm of the chair and inhaled deeply. She lifted a hand and noticed she was shaking. This was crazy! She'd recognized the hunger in his eyes, and the fact that she responded to it made it all the more powerful . . . and dangerous.

"How's your daughter?"

Amanda stuck her head out of Mike's office. Vince's head was bent as he filled out the forms.

"What did you say?" she asked.

He looked up. "I asked how your daughter was doing."

"Oh. Fine. Kim's fine."

"Have you talked to her?"

Amanda sighed. "Yes. And I need to apologize to you for being so rude. You had no way of knowing what you were doing."

"What was I doing?"

The spell broken, Amanda walked toward her desk and stood before him.

"Sheriff Messina, this is a small town. Everything that is done here is public domain. Surely you can see that bringing Kim home in a patrol car would cause a lot of senseless gossip."

Vince nodded. "I see what you mean. And you're right. I didn't give it a thought. I was only trying to help."

Amanda remembered the daughter listed in his résumé and her voice softened. "I realize that now, and I'm sorry I was so defensive. Kimberly will have a few rough days at school, but it'll blow over." She grimaced. "I know that firsthand."

"Know what firsthand?" He rose and handed her the completed forms.

She wasn't about to elaborate on her past, not now, not with him. "Forget it. Is there anything else I can do for you?"

"No. Not at the moment."

"Then, if you'll excuse me. I have to get back to work."

Vince towered over her. She certainly was a little bitty thing.

"Of course, Mrs. Simpson." He laughed. "You know, this being a small town and all, I'd really like it if you'd call me Vince."

Amanda smiled. "All right, Vince. And I'm Amanda."

He extended his hand. Reluctantly she placed her small palm next to his larger, callused one. It was warm, dry, and it completely enveloped hers. Their eyes met and held. This time, both acknowledged the attraction that was too blatant to be ignored.

"Amanda," he said softly, drawing out the word on a breath. "It's a pleasure."

After work Amanda ran across the street to the hair salon where her sister-in-law Polly worked. She'd left her car in the municipal parking lot. It had begun to act up again lately, and after spending a small fortune last month for transmission work, she was treating it with kid gloves. The car *had* to last until summer. She couldn't afford a new one; she couldn't afford to be without one, either.

"Brrr!" Polly shivered. "Close that door. It's colder out there than a—"

"Five degrees," Amanda said as she removed her coat and scarf. "Five lonely degrees, and they say it's dropping to below zero tonight."

Polly continued to tease the silver hair of old Mrs. Ballantine, who looked as if she were modeling for an ad for *Bride of Frankenstein*.

"Hello, Amanda, dear," Mrs. Ballantine said. "How are you and your family?"

Amanda stared at her frizzed head and returned her kindly smile. "Fine, Mrs. B. And you?"

"Can't complain. And even if I do, who'll listen? With Jonathan gone now, nobody talks to me anymore."

"Now that's not true," Polly said emphatically, "I talk to you every week." She continued to smooth down the tangles into a puffy bouffant.

Mrs. Ballantine patted her arm as she combed. "That's true, Polly. You're the bright spot of my week."

"There, all done."

Polly quickly lacquered the hairstyle to a stiff finish.

As the elderly woman gathered her belongings and paid the receptionist, Amanda leaned over toward Polly.

"You do that to her every week?" Amanda whispered.

"Like clockwork since 1974. The woman still wears her hair the same exact way." Polly grinned. "Don't knock it. She's my best customer!"

Amanda shook her head. "Have you time to give me a quick trim? I can't stand this hair in my eyes anymore."

"Sure. Sit down."

Mrs. Ballantine walked to Polly and handed her a tip. She bent over Amanda's seat and patted her hand. "Heard about that trouble with your girl and that Bronson boy. You'd best keep an open eye on her, Amanda. He's a troublemaker."

"Mrs. B.! Tommy's no such thing, you know that."

The old woman frowned. "Better safe than sorry, I always say." She poked Amanda's shoulder with a bony finger. "And you should know that firsthand."

She picked up her cane and headed toward the door. "Take care now, Polly. See you next week."

"Bye, now, Mrs. B.," Polly answered.

Amanda sighed as the blast of cold air hit her from the opened door. "When is this town ever going to let me forget it?"

Polly ran a comb through Amanda's curls.

"The old ones probably never will. They still think getting pregnant without being married is a fate worse than death. If it had been a boy from town instead of Billy Simpson, they more than likely would have hushed it up and forgotten all about it."

"It's been fifteen years, Polly, and I can still remember the old biddies counting on their fingers when Kimberly was born. It was the worst time of my life."

"I know," she said as she snipped Amanda's bangs. "But they never approved of Billy to begin with, and he never did make any effort to fit in."

"Oh, Polly. It's so long ago, I don't even blame Bill anymore. He felt cooped up here. In a lot of ways, it was both our faults."

"You're too good, that's the trouble. He never grew up. Dragged you and the kids all around the country, then left you to go running after that stewardess. He's living it up in sunny California, and you're stuck in Branchport raising his kids!"

"I'm not stuck. I *like* Branchport. And I like my kids. It was my choice to come back here."

"Billy asked you to go with him?"

"At first."

"Why the hell didn't you do it, then?"

When Amanda didn't answer, Polly stopped clipping.

"You didn't love him anymore, did you?" Polly asked, almost in awe.

"I . . . wouldn't say that."

"Here John and I thought you were still carrying a torch for him all these years, and you *let* him go!"

"Can we change the subject?" Amanda asked, uncomfortable, as always, talking about her past.

"Okay, okay," Polly said. "Are you all set for this weekend?"

"I agreed, didn't I? A quick movie with cousin Pete—"

"Uh, Pete's not coming."

Amanda turned in her seat. "What happened?"

"He called to cancel. He has to go out to town on business."

Amanda shrugged. "Just as well."

"But we can still double," Polly said quickly.

"Double with who? There's no one in town—"

"No one from town. Someone else. Someone new."

"New? Who could be new around here..." A cold finger of ice snaked through Amanda's insides. "The sheriff," she whispered. "You want me to go out with the sheriff."

"You guessed it! He hardly knows anybody in town. I met him in the bank today, and since Peter cancelled, I invited him. I thought it'd be the neighborly thing to do."

Her reaction to him in the office today was anything but neighborly, Amanda thought.

"I don't think so, Polly. Anyway, I'm sure he has no desire to go out with any of us."

"But he does! He said yes right away. I tell you the man was so thankful! I bet he's just bored stiff all by himself in old man Gates's fishing cottage."

"Is that where he's living?"

"Yep. And you know how deserted it is up by the lake this time of year," Polly said as she ran a brush through Amanda's hair. "So what do you say? Saturday night, the four of us? It'll be fun."

"Oh, I don't know, Polly..."

"Amanda, please...you've got to do this." Polly lowered her voice. "I already invited him. I'll look like a fool. Say yes. Come on."

Amanda felt caught between a rock and a hard place. She didn't want to be part of a foursome with the very unsettling Vince Messina, but Polly was her best friend as well as her sister-in-law.

"All right," she said quickly, before she thought better of it.

"Great! Thanks, you're an angel." She whisked the plastic covering off Amanda's lap and shook out the hair clippings. "All done. You look fabulous, as usual!"

Amanda reached for her coat and scarf and opened her purse to pay Polly.

"Keep it. It's on the house," Polly said, closing her hand over Amanda's wallet. "Wait a minute while I get my coat. I'm leaving, too. I'll walk out with you."

The two women left the shop and walked to the corner of Main Street before going their separate ways. Amanda managed a wan smile and reassured Polly that she would call to confirm the time for Saturday. She lifted the collar of her wool coat and snuggled down into the scarf as the frigid wind tossed her newly styled hair. Returning to the municipal parking lot, she stepped into her car and inserted the key into the ignition. Nothing but a faint whirring noise greeted her.

"Oh, no," she said out loud. "Not now. Please don't do this to me now!"

After three successive, unsuccessful tries, she gave up. Amanda got out of the car and lifted the hood. Why, she didn't know. Even if there was something wrong with it that could be fixed right away, she wouldn't know where to begin to look. In the years since Bill left, she'd become a pretty adept carpenter, plumber and general Ms. Fix It, but car mechanics was never a strong point of interest.

She glanced at her watch. It was almost six o'clock already, and the kids expected her home. She had dinner to cook, homework to oversee and laundry to do, not to mention a talk with Kim about her day. It wasn't fair.

Bundling the coat more securely around her, she trudged back to Main Street in search of a telephone to call Frank Stone, her mechanic. Perhaps he could come right away, give her a jump start or something. The street was practically deserted as she walked toward the diner where she knew there was a pay phone.

The warmth of the diner's foyer felt wonderful as she rubbed her gloveless hands together and proceeded to search through her purse for a quarter. As luck would have it, she found only two pennies and a nickel. She pulled out a dollar bill and entered the main room of the diner to get change.

Then she saw him.

He was sitting in the back of the dining room in a booth reading a newspaper and eating what appeared to be a hearty dinner. She stood frozen to the spot, literally and figuratively, almost willing him to look. He did, and his fork halted midway to his mouth. She watched as he slowly placed the fork on his plate, his gaze never leaving hers for a moment.

He did frightening things to her with those eyes! Amanda swallowed and turned away, handing the cashier the dollar bill and asking for change. She knew the moment he came up behind her. He didn't touch her, wasn't even standing very close to her. She just knew.

"Amanda?"

She closed her eyes tightly for a moment and turned, a bright smile on her face. "Hi!"

"Problem?"

"No, what makes you think so?"

"It's the dinner hour. You should be home by now."

"Ordinarily I would be, but I stopped for a haircut. And now, wouldn't you know it, my car won't start!"

Vince grabbed his coat from the hook by the door. "Where is it? I'll help you."

"Oh, no, please. You're having your dinner. I'll just call my mechanic. He'll be here in a jiffy. Thanks, anyway."

Amanda opened the door and walked toward the pay phone. As she lifted the receiver, a hand took hold of hers and returned it to its cradle.

"Where's the car?" he asked.

His voice was soft, sure, commanding.

"In the municipal parking lot."

Vince opened the outside door and ushered her through. "Let's go."

The wind blasted them as they walked, making small talk impossible. Amanda had to skip to keep up with his long strides. Suddenly he took hold of her arm and propelled her toward and into his car. It was a low-slung, sleek, black Corvette.

"No embarrassing squad car tonight, Mrs. Simpson," he teased.

Amanda smiled good-naturedly. "This is some car!"

"A little present to myself when I left the city."

Her car was the only one left in the lot when they arrived.

"Stay inside," he said, and slammed the car door.

Amanda watched as he lifted her car hood and fiddled with the engine. She got out of his car and bundled her scarf around her as she stood over him.

Vince looked up. "Why do I get the feeling you don't take orders well?"

She grinned. "Can you fix it?"

"It looks like it's the battery. I've got jumper cables in the trunk. Get behind the wheel and start her up when I tell you."

Vince made the proper connections, and after two attempts, the engine kicked in.

"Let it run a minute," he said.

"What can I do to thank you?" she asked as he leaned against the driver's door.

"Go out with me some night."

Amanda laughed. "I'm already going out with you, so to speak."

"What?"

"Saturday night. You agreed to go out with Polly Hatcher?"

"Yeah. Sort of, I think. She asked me to go to a movie with her and her husband. You know her?"

Amanda nodded. "She's my sister-in-law. Her husband is my brother John."

"John?"

"John Hatcher. You met him at my house Saturday."

"That was your *brother*? I thought—"

"I know what you thought."

"Why didn't you correct me?"

"I was mad." She grinned. "And you were having such a good time assuming."

Vince leaned down, his head almost filling the window on her side of the car. His eyes were sparkling, gray and searching. His full lips beckoned, invited. If she leaned forward just a little, she could kiss him. He wouldn't pull back, she knew that. Nor would she want him to. She knew that, as well.

"What time do I pick you up?" he asked.

"You don't," she answered. "I'm going with John and Polly. I'll meet you there."

"This doesn't sound like a proper date to me, Mrs. Simpson," he teased.

"It's not. So don't get any ideas." She put the car in gear, and he stepped back. "Thanks for the help," she said as she pulled away.

"Anytime," he answered to the wind. "Anytime at all."

Three

———

"Yoo-hoo! Amanda! Amanda Simpson..."

Amanda pretended not to hear. She clunked down the metal cover on top of the overflowing garbage can and grabbed the lapels of her coat together at the neck. The cold seeped through her fuzzy pink slippers and up into her body as she stood on the ice-slicked road. It had snowed two days ago. Not enough to be a major storm, just enough to be a pain. Her street had been plowed, but the thin layer that remained had been packed down into dirty ice, making walking as well as driving hazardous to one's health.

"Amanda!"

The shout had become louder, more imperative. She really, truly, couldn't pretend any longer. Gripping her unbuttoned coat tightly over her pajamas, she turned and gave an ineffective wave.

"Hi, Hester. How are you?"

Amanda looked across the street at the small A-frame and saw her neighbor's head sticking out of her front door. The white hair was set in wire curlers and wrapped with baby-blue netting, tied with a perfectly centered bow on top of her head.

"Come on over." The old woman waved. "Have a cup of coffee."

"Oh, really, Hester, I couldn't...can't...I have things—"

"Right now. Hurry, it's so cold, I can't leave the door open like this. My rheumatism, you know."

The front door slammed abruptly, and the head disappeared. Amanda sighed, trudged carefully across the ice-encrusted street and poked her head inside the door.

"Come in, come in! There you are! Sit, I've coffee all made."

Amanda smiled as she watched how spritely the poor "rheumatic" moved around the kitchen. She knew the woman was lonely and covetous of any company she could ensnare. But Amanda had grown up in this town, and she knew Hester Waterbury to be one of the worst—if not *the* worst—gossips around. She'd had to deal with her tongue many times over the years, particularly when she was married to Bill.

Still, part of Amanda felt sorry for Hester, and her natural compassion always allowed her to forgive. Over the last two years Hester had become a surrogate grandmother to Sean and Kimberly, since her own parents had moved to Florida. She never refused to baby-sit or help out with the children in any way she could, and for that Amanda was more than grateful.

Hester put a coffee cup, sugar and creamer in front of Amanda, together with freshly baked muffins.

"This is so nice of you," Amanda said. "You didn't have to go to all this trouble."

"No trouble at all, Amanda. I just baked these, and besides I haven't seen you in weeks." The elderly woman sat down across from Amanda and poured the coffee. "Now. Tell me. What's new with you?"

Amanda knew better than to say "nothing."

"Well, my car is on the fritz again. Had to have the battery recharged."

"You really should buy a new one."

"Don't I wish I could! Maybe this summer, if it holds out that long."

"You should get that Bill Simpson to pay what he owes you. I hate to see you worrying about these things."

Amanda refused to dwell on how the old woman knew her ex-husband was behind in his support payments.

"I'll be fine," she said tightly.

The old woman patted her hand. "Of course, you will. But you really should think of marrying again. Then you could stay home with your children where you belong."

"I don't want to get married again. I like working. I like my job and my life just the way it is."

Hester sighed. "I forget you young women today need something more than a home, a husband and a family to keep you busy. Why, when I was a young girl, all I wanted out of life was a home of my own and a man of my own." She took a satisfying sip of coffee and crinkled her long, pointed nose. "And, of course, I've had both."

Amanda returned a weak smile and took a bite of a muffin, more from a desire to keep her mouth busy than from a desire for food.

"All that trouble with Kimberly and that Bronson boy over with?" Hester asked sweetly.

Amanda gagged on her muffin. She took a sip of coffee to wash it down and burnt her tongue. The woman did it to her every time. It seemed to be one of her top ten pleasures in life—to catch her off-guard.

"There was no trouble. It was all a misunderstanding."

"That's not what I heard," the old woman said, nodding her head for emphasis. "It was shoplifting, all right. Heard it straight from Liddy Halverson."

Liddy's husband, Sam, was one of Branchport's deputies. She worked across the way from Amanda in the tax assessor's office, which was conveniently in the same building as the police station. Liddy and Amanda had gone to school together, but there had never been any love lost between them. It was no wonder she was the one to spread the news about Kim. Amanda wanted a quick end to this conversation.

"Well, you heard wrong. I spoke to the sheriff myself, and everything is cleared up."

"Take my advice, Amanda, and keep Kimberly away from that Bronson boy. He's trouble. This isn't the first time he's been involved in this sort of thing."

Amanda finished her coffee and pushed the cup away. "What do you mean?"

"Tommy Bronson has been picked up twice for the very same thing, oh, a year or so ago. Odus kept a record, but never charged the boy because of his age. Didn't that new sheriff tell you?"

"No." Amanda frowned. "He never mentioned it."

"Probably had his mind on other things." She shook her head disparagingly and leaned forward. "City people," she stated, as if that said it all. "Hear he's good-looking, though." She eyed Amanda over the rim of her coffee cup. "And single."

It was time to go. Amanda had no desire to discuss the new sheriff with anyone, least of all Hester Waterbury. She stood and buttoned her coat.

"Oh, look at the time. I've really got to go. Thanks for the coffee. See you soon."

She was down the hall and out the door before the poor woman could follow. Amanda was halfway across the street, when Hester's head poked out the door.

"Come visit again soon, Amanda. Don't be a stranger!"

Amanda waved without turning, opened the front door and slammed it shut. She leaned against the hard wood and closed her eyes.

The more she thought about it, the more she realized what folly it was to go through with tonight. She was undeniably attracted to Vince Messina, and it was not only foolish to double-date with him, it was dangerous. Once it got around town that she was seen with him, there would be a rash of gossip about the two of them. It had been a long time since she was the topic of everyone's conversation, and that was fine with her.

That naive teenage girl who fell for an out-of-town jock was all grown up now, a mother and a respected member of the community. So why was she beginning to feel a rumbling inside, as if a sleeping giant were awakening?

The image of Vince Messina and his penetrating eyes flashed across her mind, and her insides tightened in anticipation. Mature or not, she had to admit she was as excited—and apprehensive—as a young girl on her first date.

"Mom? Where's my white blouse? You know, the one with the bow around the collar? I can't find it," Kim called from upstairs.

"Check again. It's hanging in your closet."

Amanda pushed herself away from the door and unbuttoned her coat, hanging it on the bentwood rack in the hallway. With Kim at a party tonight and Sean sleeping over at Cory's, Amanda couldn't think of an excuse to cancel. The thought of being with Vince intensified the churning in the pit of her stomach, and she knew if she was honest with herself, she didn't want to find an excuse. Because when all was said and done, she really wanted to go. Not for the movie, not even for John and Polly.

She wanted to see him again.

The theater was dark. The projector flickered and flashed bright blasts of light across the screen as the opening credits rolled to the blare of background music. They had just made it. John and Polly had been late to pick her up and they'd had to rush to be on time. They'd met Vince by the snack counter and had hurried in to find seats before the show began. Amanda had been glad for the lack of time. It had solved the problem of the initial awkward small talk she had been dreading all day.

Vince held out the extra-large cardboard tub of buttered popcorn toward her. She grabbed a handful and muttered her thanks.

The theater was crowded, and because they were late, the two couples had to split up. Amanda was sandwiched between Vince and a group of teenage boys

who were commenting on every little thing happening
on the screen. She felt confined and uncomfortable as
she sat on her coat in the narrow seat and tried to ignore the boys, their raucous remarks and their constant
fidgeting.

As the credits rolled off the screen and the movie
began, Vince leaned across her and tapped the teenage
boy next to her on the shoulder.

"Cool it."

His voice was soft but commanding. His face was
only inches away from hers, but he didn't turn toward
her. She studied his profile in the semidarkness and
willed him to look at her. He didn't, but continued to
stare at the group to her left. In turn, each boy stopped
talking, dropped his feet from the seat in front of him,
and sat up in the cushioned chairs.

Vince nodded and leaned back.

"Very impressive," she whispered.

He glanced her way with what could have been a
smile, but seemed more like a tolerant smirk. "Years
of practice." He took her hand and squeezed it, then,
without releasing it from his grasp, held it high on his
thigh as he returned his attention to the screen.

Amanda didn't know what to do. At thirty-four she
hadn't been out on a date since high school. And even
though this wasn't really a *date*, she still felt self-
conscious holding his hand.

She didn't know how to act with a man anymore, but
then, did she ever? She and Billy had married a few
months after her high school graduation. Her years of
being a wife, mother and single parent did nothing to
prepare her for this. She remembered the excitement of
those innocent first dates, but she had been a young girl
then, ignorant of life and what it had to offer. She stole

a quick glance at Vince, and her insides quivered with a mixture of anticipation and fear; she wasn't that young girl anymore.

Amanda squirmed in her seat and crossed her legs in the confined space. As she did, her ankle brushed Vince's knee.

"Sorry," she whispered, and moved her leg.

"No problem," he said, finally turning to look her in the eye. "Keep it there."

Those gray eyes possessed a silver luster in the false light. Amanda's heart skipped a beat; he made her feel nervous, jumpy... wonderful.

"You're not watching the movie," she whispered softly.

"No," he answered.

She forced herself to turn away, begging her eyes to focus and concentrate on the story unfolding on the screen. It was a suspense tale, and all the rage with the critics. She had wanted to see the movie for weeks, and now she found herself too absorbed with the movements of the man next to her to know or care about what was taking place on the screen.

A side glance told her he was slowly, laboriously, savoring each piece of popcorn in his mouth. She watched as his cheeks contracted, and knew he was rolling his tongue around it, toying with it, melting it within the heat of his mouth.

Her own began to salivate.

Without moving his eyes from the screen, Vince offered her the tub once again. *He knows I'm watching him,* she thought, *and he likes it.* Determined, Amanda pulled her gaze from him and fixed her attention to the screen.

Before long she was involved in the story, lost to all around her. When the hero kissed the heroine deeply and laid her on the bed, Amanda's throat went dry. She felt the heat in her face as the couple on the screen rolled around in seminaked splendor. There was nothing lewd about the scene. It was tastefully done, but the temperature in the theater rose significantly, and she dared not look at Vince.

The moans and heavy breathing continued as the two actors did a very believable job of making love. Amanda looked down for a moment, as embarrassed as she was fascinated. Her peripheral vision caught Vince watching her. She turned her head slowly and was hit full force with the power of his sexuality. Vince's face was taut, his eyes bright, and his lips full. Amanda felt her nipples tighten beneath her heavy woolen sweater. She licked her lips and his heavy-lidded gaze followed the movement to her mouth, saying more with a look than a thousand words ever could. She removed her hand from his and rubbed her moist palm against her thigh, and together they watched the back-and-forth motion of her hand. A warm tingling swept her lower body, and she squeezed her legs together in defense.

The scene on the screen shifted to a loud car chase, piercing the almost sacred silence of the theater with a police siren. The lovemaking was over up there, but her heart still pounded down here.

The rest of the movie went by uneventfully, as she refused to look his way again. This was ridiculous, insane, and she couldn't—wouldn't—give in to those instincts again.

"Wasn't that great?" Polly said as they stood on the sidewalk outside the movie theater. "Especially the part in the hotel room!"

Amanda watched her sister-in-law hang on to John's arm as he returned her dreamy smile.

"Well," Amanda said, "it's late. I'd better be getting home."

"What's the hurry, Amanda? It's only ten o'clock. Let's go for a drink or something," John said.

"Yeah," Polly joined in. "Let's go dancing over at Buzzard's."

Amanda shook her head. "I'm in no mood for Buzzard's."

"Don't be a party pooper." Polly pouted. "You haven't been there in years. The place has changed, hasn't it, John?"

"What's Buzzard's?" Vince asked.

"It used to be a shot-and-a-beer joint down at the edge of town. Pretty rough crowd. But it changed hands last year, and the new owners are trying for a more upscale clientele," John said. "It's not much, but they do have a great oldies jukebox."

"Sounds like fun," Vince said. The jukebox did it. The place might not be as trendy as those he was used to, but any excuse right now to hold Amanda in his arms was incentive enough for him.

All eyes turned to Amanda.

"All right! Let's go to Buzzard's."

The stifling air of a crowded, smoke-filled room greeted them as they entered Buzzard's. People were three-deep at the bar, and all of the tables looked occupied. A small parquet dance floor took up one corner of a room that had a variety of plants hanging from the ceiling. An old-fashioned jukebox blasted a mournful rock-a-billy song as couples swayed in time to the rhythm.

Scanning the room, Vince noticed a few of the rough customers John had referred to leaning against the corner of the bar and guzzling beer straight from the bottle. He instinctively put his arm around Amanda as they made their way through the crowd.

"Look," John shouted above the din and pointed to the opposite end. "Those people look as if they're leaving. Let's grab their table."

After they were seated, a harried waitress managed to push her way over to take their order.

"What'll you have?" she asked.

"Carafe of white wine okay with everyone?" John asked.

"You go ahead," Vince said, then turned to the waitress. "Coke for me. Lots of ice."

John gave the wine order, and then he and Polly got up to dance. The music blared and Amanda leaned closer to Vince.

"Don't you drink?"

"Wine with dinner, beer at home, but for the most part, no. I learned a long time ago it's not too bright to drink when you're carrying."

"Carrying what?"

He opened his jacket just enough for her to see the leather strap of his gun holster. Amanda stared for a moment with a combination of fascination and revulsion.

"Oh," she said. "Do you carry it with you all the time? Even when you're out socially?"

Vince nodded. "For the most part."

"Why?"

"Because you don't stop being a cop just because you're off duty. And too many times you see something happening that needs taking care of right away."

"Doesn't it bother you," she asked, "to know that any time, day or night, you might have to be involved with someone violent?"

Vince shook his head. "It's not a nine-to-five job, Amanda. It's a way of life. You know that from the start." It was important that she understand this about him. He was a cop, inside and out. It was an integral part of him. He searched her eyes for her true reaction to his statement.

Amanda was a bit startled by the intensity of his words. "I give you a lot of credit to be able to live that way. I know I couldn't. Just the thought of using that—" she pointed to the side of his jacket where his gun lay hidden "—would scare me to death."

"I've been doing it for almost twenty years now. I guess I'm used to it. But I understand how you feel."

He brought his hand up to massage the back of her neck, and she relaxed against the warm pressure. She watched his face and saw a cloud pass over his eyes. She wondered what he was thinking about. She was tempted to ask, when a classic Fifties rendition of "Only You" began playing on the jukebox.

"Dance with me," he said so softly she had to read his lips.

Amanda put her arm around him as they found a small space on the dance floor. Vince entwined his fingers with hers and held them down on his thigh as their bodies touched. She stared up into his eyes and melted against him as a weakness spread through her. Vince let go of her hand and wrapped both arms around her waist, and she followed suit. They fit together perfectly, moving slowing to the music. The heat of the room and the words of the song transported them into a world all their own.

"What are you doing to me?" He seemed to be asking himself more than her.

"The same thing you're doing to me, I'm afraid," she answered.

"Are you?"

"Am I what?"

"Afraid?"

"Yes, very much," she whispered.

"Me, too."

Vince bent his head and brushed his full lips lightly against hers. Their warm breath mingled. More than anything else right now, she wanted him to kiss her. She wanted to taste him, feel his mouth on hers. She wanted it so much, she was trembling.

The music ended, and the other couples leaving the dance floor jostled them as a fast rock song shattered the mood. Vince and Amanda returned to their seats and exchanged small talk with Polly and John. The bar was becoming more noisy and crowded, if that was possible. She checked her watch and excused herself to find a phone to call to see if Kim was home from her party yet.

The phone rang five times. She was just about to hang up when Kim answered.

"Hello," she sounded out of breath.

"Hi," Amanda said, "it's me. Did you just get in?"

"Just this minute, Mom. I ran when I heard the phone."

"How was the party?"

"Great," Kim answered.

Amanda heard mumbling in the background. "Who's there with you?"

"Oh, Tommy walked me home."

Amanda felt a surge of annoyance. She mentally counted to ten.

"Kimberly, we've talked about this. You know how I feel. Tell him to leave. It's late."

"I know, I know. He's just going."

"I'm on my way home now. Be sure he's gone when I get there."

"Problem?"

Amanda cradled the phone, turned and confronted Vince.

"Why didn't you tell me Tommy Bronson had been picked up for shoplifting twice before?" she asked.

"I didn't know about it when I dropped Kim off that day. But even if I did, I wouldn't have told you. Where did you hear it?"

"Does it matter?"

Vince shook his head and glanced at the ceiling in annoyance. "In this town? Probably not."

"What's that supposed to mean?"

"You people have a hell of a grapevine."

"There's good and bad in that statement, Sheriff," Amanda said. "People here care about one another and help one another, not like the city where they step over bodies in the street."

She turned her back to him and started to make her way to the table. Amanda was more than annoyed. She'd spent what sometimes seemed like a lifetime defending Branchport to Billy and was sick to death of people denigrating her town.

Vince caught up with her and spun her around to face him. "Hey, I'm sorry. I didn't mean to insult you or the town. The people here have been great to me. I'm just not used to it."

Amanda sighed. "I know." She pulled her arm from his grasp. "I'm sorry I snapped at you. But I need to get John. Kim's back from her party, and I have to leave."

"They're having a good time." He motioned to John and Polly on the dance floor. "Let them stay. I'll take you home."

"You don't have—"

"I want to."

Vince indicated to John that they were leaving. Amanda waved to her brother as they walked out the door. The air was cold, crisp and invigorating after the overheated atmosphere of the club. Vince held the door for her as she slipped into the passenger seat of the Corvette.

During the short ride home they shared a tense silence. Amanda had to admit she was attracted to him. She also was convinced there was no future for them. His apology notwithstanding, he had the same condescending attitude about Branchport that Billy had. They were from two different worlds and wanted two different things. She'd had fun tonight, there was no doubt about that. And if that dance they shared was any indication of his feelings, he'd want to see her again.

But nothing could ever come of it. He was only here for a couple of months. She couldn't afford to become involved with someone like him, someone who would be easy to fall in love with. Where would she be then? No, she told herself, better to stop it now, nip it in the bud. Her life was nice, neat and happy.

How about satisfying? a little voice murmured in her ear. Amanda ignored it.

Within ten minutes they were in front of her house. Out of habit, Amanda glanced across the street to Hester Waterbury's, but the house was dark and the blinds on the front window safely shut for the night.

Amanda didn't wait for him to open the car door. She walked slowly to her house and climbed the two steps onto the porch. Fiddling with her keys, she turned and waited as he followed behind. Vince stopped on the gravel at the bottom of the porch. He placed one foot on the first step and leaned forward toward her.

"Thank you, Vince," Amanda said. "I did have a nice time tonight."

"So did I," he said softly, then paused. "I want to see you again, Amanda."

She shook her head. "I don't think that would be a good idea. For either of us."

"Why?"

"I'm not really interested in dating."

"Dating at all? Or just dating me?"

"Does it matter?"

He looked hurt, and part of her wanted to console him. But she felt she had no choice. To see him again would be too dangerous. She'd been on her own a long time, and was proud of her ability to take care of herself and her children. Five years without a man in her life had not been the easiest way to live, but it was safe.

She looked into his luminous gray eyes and, for a moment, questioned the value of safety when all was said and done.

Vince studied each feature on her face, his gaze stopping at her eyes. The disappointment was heavy in his chest, and he swallowed to assuage the unexpected ache. He was annoyed with himself that her refusal to see him affected him so, but he wouldn't push. It wasn't his style.

"Okay," he said softly. The gravel under his feet crunched as he took a retreating step. "If you change your mind, you know where I am."

Amanda suppressed a longing to reach out and touch him. "I still hope we can be friends, Vince."

He ran a hand through his hair and laughed out loud, a sardonic sound filled with remorse. "No—" he shook his head "—no, I don't think so."

Unexpectedly he moved onto the step, leaned over and gave her a quick, hard kiss on the lips.

"Not friends, Amanda. Never friends."

Four

———

So, did he kiss you?'' Polly asked as she flipped the left directional signal and turned the car onto Main Street.

Amanda ignored her. Since their infamous double date, Polly had done nothing except question her about Vince Messina. Irritation and something else she wouldn't name warred inside her every time the subject came up. She usually changed the subject, but try as she might, Amanda could not get that night, or the man, out of her mind. Polly's constant chatter about how great they looked together only added fuel to an already smoldering fire.

''Well, did he?''

Amanda sighed, then shrugged as she looked away from Polly and out the passenger window. ''Sort of.''

''What do you mean, sort of? What's a 'sort of' kiss?''

''A short, quick kiss.''

"Maybe he kisses everyone like that," Polly suggested.

"Actually, it wasn't a kiss at all. It was more of a kiss-off."

"I don't get it. He seemed real interested in you."

"He is."

"Well, then?"

"*I'm* not interested."

"Amanda Simpson, you're crazy! The guy's the best thing ever to happen to this town, besides being gorgeous. And you're not interested in him?"

"I didn't say I wasn't interested in *him*. I'm not interested in what *he's* interested in."

"And that is . . . ?"

"An affair. A quick, brief, probably disgustingly earthy affair."

Polly chuckled. "Sounds okay to me."

Amanda returned a dirty look. "Well, it's not what I want."

"Thinking about holding out for a ring this time?"

Amanda laughed out loud. "You know, if anyone else ever said that to me, I'd probably punch them in the nose."

"You didn't answer my question."

Amanda grew pensive. "Yeah. Maybe I am. Anything wrong with that?"

"No." Polly shook her head. "Nothing wrong. Only that you're not eighteen anymore. And he sure as hell isn't Billy Simpson."

Polly stopped the car in front of the municipal center, and Amanda stepped out.

"Thanks for the ride," she said.

"When's your car going to be ready?"

Amanda made a face. The old shebang was on its last leg. She had to get a new car, and soon. She expected a decent tax return and hoped it would be enough for a down payment.

"Frank Stone said it's the alternator. He should have it fixed today. I can walk over to his place after work."

"Call if you change your mind and need a ride, okay?"

"Okay. Thanks again."

Amanda slammed the car door and headed into the center. She made a mental note to call Bill in California tonight about those late support payments. In the last year or so, she had stopped bugging him about it and made do; but she needed a car, and as much as she hated having to ask him for anything, there was nowhere else to turn for the money.

A message was on her desk to join the mayor in his office as soon as she arrived. *Wouldn't you know it,* she thought, *the one day I'm late is the one day he's looking for me.* Amanda took a legal-size pad out of her top drawer and picked up her Cross pen. Her heels tapped out a rhythm as she made her way across the tiled floor to Mike's office. She knocked and opened the door.

"Sorry I'm late, Mike," she said. "My car broke down again and—"

"No problem, Amanda, we're just getting started." Her boss pointed to a chair for her to be seated. "You know Sheriff Messina, don't you?"

Amanda twisted before her bottom hit the chair, suddenly noticing the man standing between the large fern and the window. Her heart skipped a beat; he was the last person she expected to see here this morning. A warm flush crept over her body at the sight of him.

"Of course. Sheriff..." She nodded, quickly turning her attention back to her boss. "What's this all about, Mike?"

"You've heard about these robberies that have been taking place around town, haven't you?"

"Yes, I've been reading about them. The video store, the stationery store, a few homes in the area. The newspaper implied it was kids."

"It's not kids," Vince interjected.

Amanda focused on him. "Then who is it?"

"I don't know. Yet. But these robberies were carried out by professionals. Nothing sloppy about them."

"The sheriff thought it wise for us to warn the Chamber of Commerce members to take some extra security measures, particularly the bank," Mike said.

"Surely you don't think they would be so bold as to try to rob the bank!" Amanda said.

"No," Vince said, "I don't. From what we've put together, there's more than one person involved, and they know what they're doing. The stores were hit at night, and the private homes when the occupants were out." He tucked a thumb in a belt loop. "They study their prey before striking and seem to know what's going on in town."

"You think someone from town is involved?" she asked.

Vince shrugged. "Could be. I don't know. Someone could be involved and not even know it."

Mike shook his head. "How can that be, Sheriff?"

"Easy. People like to talk around here—" he looked at Amanda "—or so I've been told. There's a distinct routine to the businesses in this town, as well as for the people. Someone who knows all of that can be very helpful to a thief."

"So what you want the businesses to do is change their routine?" Mike asked.

"Yes. Continue business as usual, but ask them to choose different times or different ways to make their deposits. I don't want people walking around with large sums of money making night deposits until this thing is cleared up."

"Sounds like a good idea to me," Mike said. "Amanda? Can you make those calls?"

"Certainly. We have at least a half dozen businesses in town that do just that. I'll make up a suggested schedule and contact them today." Amanda rose. "Is that all, Sheriff?"

Vince stared at her for an exceedingly long moment before answering. She was nervously aware of Mike's presence, but refused to break eye contact until he did.

"For now," Vince said, and turned toward the door to open it, expecting Amanda to precede him.

"Thanks, Sheriff," Mike said as they left. "Let me know anything else we can do to help."

"Will do. I'll be in touch."

Amanda was alarmingly aware of him as he walked her back to her desk. She put down the pen and pad and looked up at him. For the first time she noticed how tired and drawn he looked, as if he hadn't slept in a while.

"You look exhausted," she said, concern apparent in her voice despite her attempt to hide it.

Vince ran a hand over his face. "I'm beat. These robberies have been keeping us busy. Sam and I've been splitting double shifts with the other deputies handling everything else. If we don't crack this soon, I'm going to have to get some outside help."

"You need some rest. You look awful."

Vince grinned. "Thanks for the compliment. But you're right. I'm off duty now and going home to sleep the day away."

"Let me know if there is anything else I can do for you," she said.

He stared at her again with that same penetrating look that peeled away the layers of indifference she'd tried to build against him.

"You know what you can do for me," he whispered.

A chill ran down her back at the raspy promise in his voice, and she closed her eyes to break the contact.

"You never give up, do you? I hope you're this diligent in your work, Sheriff," she said.

Vince laughed and squinted his eyes. "Never fear, Mrs. Simpson, I always get my man." He leaned over the desk and brought his face within inches of hers. "And my woman."

He rapped the desk with his knuckles, graced her with a devilish grin, turned and entered the hallway. She didn't want to watch him leave; she wanted to sit down at her desk and begin her work, totally unconcerned and unbothered by him. But her eyes refused to stray from his broad back, or his well-rounded, tightly muscled buttocks. The night stick swung back and forth on his left, and his revolver was strapped securely to his right thigh. Polly was right. He was gorgeous.

Amanda saw Liddy Halverson and Vince exchange pleasantries on his way out the door. As she was about to turn away, she saw Liddy give an appreciative backward glance. A sudden, sharp stab of jealousy blindsided her.

Amanda blinked and swallowed. *Where did that come from?* She'd never been the possessive type, not even with Billy when she'd had good reason to be. It always seemed such a nuisance to have to check up on him, as if he were another child that needed to be kept in line.

So this reaction to Vince caught her completely off guard. She had no claims to him, no right to feel this way. He was a handsome, virile man, and certainly other women were going to look at him. He'd probably even date while he was in town.

The thought made her nauseous.

She told herself to stop being silly, get back to work. She'd made up her mind, had, in fact, been very firm and to the point with him: she didn't want anything to do with him. Whom or what he dated was no concern of hers.

"Seems like a nice enough fellow."

Amanda blinked and focused on Mike Powell standing next to her. She hadn't even heard his approach.

"Yes," she said, disoriented. "He does."

"We were lucky to get him. He has an impressive record in New York as a tough street cop. Heard he was involved in a lot of the big page-one stories." Mike rocked on his heels.

Amanda nodded in response. She wondered if those shadows that occasionally clouded Vince's face had anything to do with those "page-one" stories. She was very attracted to him; there was no doubt about it. Yet he was truly a stranger, and she was also curious about him, his life and why he'd come to Branchport. She shook her head. It didn't do any good to dwell on him or his past. Because, she reminded herself, there would not—could not—be a future for either of them.

"I'd better start making those calls," she said.

"Oh, yeah, sure. Let me know if you need any help. I'll contact Statler over at the bank and tell him what's going on."

Amanda lifted the receiver and heard the dial tone, but for all her self-lecturing, the only vision in her mind was that of Vince going home, shedding his clothes and climbing into bed.

One of these days, she thought, *I'm going to listen to the weather report.* The snow flurries swirled around her as Amanda threw her scarf over her shoulder and made her way down the street toward Polly's shop. She'd left the office at five o'clock with every intention of walking the half mile or so to Frank Stone's gas station. But the combination of snow and her sensible two-inch heels changed her mind. She skidded all the way to the shop and poked her head inside.

"Polly here?" she asked the receptionist.

"No, she had some shopping to do. She left a little while ago. Want to leave a message?"

Amanda sighed. "No. Forget it. Thanks anyway."

She pulled up her collar and began her trek down Main Street, walking cautiously as she counted each step in an attempt to take her mind off the cold. She turned on Clancey Street, slipping and sliding down the slight incline to the bottom and made a left onto Maple Drive. She was off the main drag now and in the old part of town. Branchport had been around since before the American Revolution, and some of the houses near the lake north of Main Street were historic landmarks that had been preserved. It was a quiet part of town, and one Amanda always liked to walk through, especially in the spring when the old, towering oak trees that lined the streets began to bloom.

Today, however, was not one of those days. She cut through Maple to Poplar, a shortcut she knew would eliminate a few blocks.

She was almost on top of the police car before she saw it. The snow was falling harder now, and the little daylight that was left was fading fast. Vince was standing on the front porch of the old Prine house where two elderly sisters lived alone. He appeared to be knocking and talking to himself at the same time. *What was he doing here?* she wondered, and quickened her pace, stopping at the white picket fence.

"I thought you were going to sleep the day away, Sheriff?"

Vince was surprised to see Amanda appear as if from nowhere. He knew she was unaware of the picture she presented standing there like an angel in a whirlpool of fine white flakes.

It made him feel warm just to look at her. He didn't know why she'd triggered this joy, but the sight of her always served as a balm to his raw emotions. He was feeling too much, much too much for her, he knew that. Her sweetness and yes, even purity for all her marriage and motherhood, filled him with a contentment he'd forgotten existed. He wanted her in his life as much as he wanted her in his bed; and that was a sobering thought, for Vince had stopped thinking in terms of permanence long ago.

"What are you doing here?" he asked.

Amanda blew a snowflake off her upper lip. "Walking to get my car at the gas station. What are you up to with the Prine sisters? I thought you were off duty."

"Sam called me at home. Seems these ladies were robbed last Friday night and spent all this time trying to decide whether to call the police or not. I've knocked several times, and I know they're in there, but they won't answer the door."

Amanda climbed the steps and stood next to him on the porch.

"They're nervous old ladies. Lorna was married for forty years. She moved back in with her sister Majorie after her husband died two years ago. They don't go out much anymore. Want me to try?"

Vince extended his hand toward the door knocker. "Be my guest."

"Miss Prine? Mrs. Macahan?" Amanda called as she knocked. "It's me, Amanda Simpson. Open up."

Vince and Amanda waited a moment, and then noticed the curtain being pulled back from the window on the left side of the door. A small wrinkled finger was visible through the pane.

"Amanda? Is that really you?" a wobbly voice asked.

"Yes," Amanda shouted. "Open up, please. I'm here with the sheriff. He wants to ask you some questions."

The door creaked open, and the light and warmth of the small home spilled out. Lorna Macahan pulled her woolen cardigan tighter around her frail chest, and eyed the man standing beside Amanda as if he were an ax murderer instead of an officer of the law.

"Mrs. Macahan, this is Sheriff Vincent Messina. He wants to talk to you about the robbery."

"Don't look like no sheriff to me," she said. "Where's Odus Tucker?"

"Odus Tucker is still recuperating from his heart attack, ma'am," Vince said softly. "He'll be back as soon as he's able."

Lorna looked from Amanda to Vince and back again. "You sure he is who he says he is?"

Amanda nodded. "Yes, I'm sure."

"Then come on in," the old woman said as she ushered them into the parlor. "Can't be too careful these days, you know. I read the papers and watch that television set right over there. I know all about those killers who dress up like plumbers and telephone men—" she turned and gave Vince a thorough once-over "—and even policemen!"

"You're right to be careful, ma'am. Here—" he handed her his badge and identification "—look it over."

Lorna picked up her reading glasses from the coffee table and slipped them onto the tip of her nose, carefully examining his credentials. Satisfied, she returned them to him, motioning for them to sit.

"Sam tells me you called to report a robbery," Vince began. "Can you tell me what happened?"

Lorna sat back in the Queen Anne chair and straightened her collar. "Well, it happened Friday night."

Vince nodded and waited for her to continue. When it was clear that she was finished with her explanation, he glanced at Amanda, only to see her suppressing a smile.

"Friday night is bingo night at the American Legion Hall," Amanda explained. "Mrs. Macahan and her sister *always* go to bingo on Friday night."

"I see," he said. "And everyone in town knows that, I assume?"

"Yes, of course," said Lorna. "We've been going for forty years, at the very least."

Vince smiled at the old woman. "Can you tell me what was taken?"

"Money from the cookie jar, some jewelry and, of course, the brooch."

"The brooch?" he asked.

"Yes, Grandmother's brooch. Pre-Civil War. Ivory cameo set in gold. Antique and very beautiful." Lorna raised her chin. "Of course, it's not mine. It's Majorie's. Why Mama left it to her I'll never know. I'm the oldest!"

"Mama promised it to me when I was only a little girl!" a voice squeaked from the hallway.

"Stop hiding, Majorie Prine," Lorna scolded. "And come in. Sheriff, this is my sister," she said as a frail, thin, white-haired woman entered the room.

Majorie's lips were pursed. "She left it to me because she knew I'd take good care of it."

"Humph!" said Lorna. "Such good care that now it's gone!"

Majorie burst into tears, the copious drops wetting her tiny face. "How can you say such a thing to me? It wasn't my fault. It wasn't!"

Vince looked at Amanda, his eyes wide with shock and concern. Amanda shook her head slightly, a tolerant and somewhat amused look on her face. He got the message that this outburst was business as usual for the sisters, and returned the grin. He'd had about enough. He'd get Sam to come out tomorrow and dust for fingerprints, but from the looks of the highly polished furniture, he had a feeling they'd come up empty.

"Thank you, ladies, for your help." He stood. "May I check the doors and windows before I leave?"

Majorie was still sobbing, but her elder sister chose to ignore her. "Of course, go right ahead."

Vince walked the house as Amanda tried to comfort Majorie. "Don't worry, Miss Prine. I'm sure the sheriff will do everything possible to get that brooch and all your belongings back to you."

"I hope so," she sobbed, "Mama wanted me to keep it forever."

"Bah! Pay no attention to her!" Lorna said.

Vince returned to the parlor and caught Amanda's eye. She met him at the front door as he checked the lock for signs of entry.

"Amanda," Lorna said, "you must come for tea some afternoon."

Amanda smiled. "I'd love to, but I work now. No more afternoon teas, I'm afraid."

"You should find a nice young man and get married again." She leaned forward and whispered, "This one seems fine."

Vince's head shot up, and his gaze locked with Amanda's embarrassed one.

"I—I don't think so, Mrs. Macahan."

Lorna patted her hand. "Well, it was good to see you, dear. Say hello to your parents for me. Why I haven't seen your mother and father since—"

"Goodbye, ma'am," Vince interrupted. "Sam Halverson will be by tomorrow to check some things with you."

Lorna nodded. "Nice to meet you, young man. And make sure you catch this culprit. Majorie won't rest until that brooch is returned, and as you can see—" she motioned to her still-sobbing sister "—neither will I."

The door closed behind them. Vince and Amanda waited for the lock to click before looking at each other.

"I've got to tell you," he said, shaking his head slowly. "I've met some characters in my twenty years on the force, but those two..."

"When poor old Majorie started crying, the expression on your face was priceless." Amanda looked at her watch. "Oh, Lord! It's after six, I've got to get home. Kimberly is making dinner tonight. She'll be calling all over town looking for me."

It was dark now, and the snow was falling heavily, the street and sidewalk completely covered. Amanda grabbed hold of the wooden railing and stepped down into the snow that covered the top of her shoe.

Vince came up behind and wrapped his right arm around her, guiding her toward the squad car. "Get in before you get soaked. I'll take you to the gas station."

"I've never been in a police car before," she said as he started the engine.

"I should hope not. Is the car at Stone's?"

"Yes. The poor man must be wondering what happened to me. I told him I'd be there around five."

"Why were you walking? Couldn't you get a ride from someone?"

Amanda sighed. "Polly offered, but I forgot to call her, and she was gone by the time I got to her shop."

Vince pulled into the gas station. It was deserted, and the doors were locked.

"Looks like Frank's left for the day."

"He can't have! I've got to get my car!"

"I'll drive you home," Vince said. He extended his arm and leaned over the seat for a better view as he began to back the car out.

The glow from the station's floodlights illuminated his face as their eyes met and held. Vince hit the brakes, and the car skidded to a halt. His gaze locked with hers before he pushed the gear into park. They sat silently, staring, communicating feelings Amanda felt were best left unsaid.

She was all too aware of the charged atmosphere in the car, aware of the heat in his eyes, the promise of his heavy-lidded gaze; but for the life of her, she couldn't turn away. She studied his mouth, those full lips that enticed her from the first. She remembered that short hard kiss at her front door. Polly's words came to mind, and she couldn't help wondering if he did indeed kiss everyone like that.

"Amanda—"

"I want you to know I don't mind if you date someone in town."

Amanda felt her face flush. *Why did she say that?* Because it had been on her mind all day.

Vince grinned. "Gee, thanks. But I didn't know I needed your permission."

"I—I wasn't implying that you did. It's just that—"

"I'm not interested in dating anyone in town." He leaned toward her. "I want you."

"Don't say that."

"Why not? It's true. I want you so bad I can taste it, Amanda."

He was almost on top of her now. She didn't pull back, even when she felt his breath on her face. She did raise her head, however, and her lips parted in anticipation.

And then he kissed her. A real kiss this time, a kiss she knew she'd never forget.

His mouth was warm, so warm that when it touched hers a bittersweet shaft of pleasure-pain shot through her system. Amanda closed her eyes as he deepened the kiss, opening her mouth with his tongue as it entered and slowly explored the inside of her own. Her heart and head began to pound in tandem, and she couldn't seem to get enough air into her lungs.

Yet it never dawned on her to push away. The touch of him was as vital as the air for which she fought. She raised her hand and placed her palm on his chest, partly for support, partly giving in to the need to feel him.

Vince broke away, and rolled his roughened cheek against her smooth one so that only the corners of their mouths touched. "Oh God," he said, "tell me I'm not crazy. Tell me this is really happening. Tell me you feel it, too."

"Yes..." she answered. "Yes..."

His mouth covered hers once again, and this time his arms came around her, pulling her into him, crushing her to him. She felt his heart pound against her as she ran a hand through his thick hair.

A motor revved behind them, and they jumped away from each other simultaneously. In silence, eyes locked, they sat, trying to understand what just happened. Neither spoke; neither knew what to say.

Amanda took a deep breath and opened the car door. Vince captured her wrist in his hand, holding her in place. She turned to see Frank Stone stepping out of his pickup truck.

He waved. "That you, Mrs. Simpson?"

"Yes, Frank," she called, surprised at how normal her voice sounded.

"Car's ready. Hang on a minute, and I'll open up the garage doors and pull it out for you."

"Thanks," she said, then returned her attention to Vince. She tugged at her wrist in his grip. "I have to go."

"Go out with me."

"I can't."

"Saturday night."

"No," she said as she watched the mechanic back her car out of the garage and walk toward her once again.

"Let me go, please. He's coming over."

"Saturday night."

"I told you I can't. I have to—"

"Friday, then. Seven o'clock."

"Mrs. Simpson . . . ?" Frank called.

Amanda looked Vince directly in the eye. "Seven-thirty."

She pulled at her wrist, and he released her just as the mechanic arrived at the car door. The man leaned over and peered inside.

"Hi ya, Sheriff."

"Frank," Vince added by way of a greeting.

Amanda left the car and secured her scarf around her neck. "Thanks for the ride, Sheriff," she said.

"Anytime, Mrs. Simpson," Vince said politely. He put the car in gear and pulled away, giving a short beep of the horn as a farewell.

"Not a bad guy, that new sheriff," Frank commented as he collected his payment from Amanda.

"No," Amanda replied.

Not a bad kisser, either.

Five

Vince stood at the edge of the lake and stared at the frozen expanse. The light from the cottage spilled out of the window illuminating the well-worn dirt path. He shrugged his shoulders to ward off a chill as a gust of February wind swept across the lake.

The cold cleared his head, and he welcomed it. With an almost imperceptible shake of his head, he mocked himself with a smile. Like it or not, he was nervous about tonight. After all those nights on the streets of New York in uniform and out, a small-town date with a pint-sized woman had accomplished what true danger never could.

Amanda posed a new and interesting problem. He didn't feel particularly smug about it, but he'd never met a woman who'd refused him before. He was forced to think about what he wanted from her.

Jamming his hands into his pants pocket, he kicked a loose stone onto the ice. Hell, there was nothing to think about. He wanted her. He wanted to make love with her, slowly, thoroughly, all night long. And no matter what she said, she wanted it, too. Did it matter so much that he would only be in town a short time?

He started back up the path and returned to the warmth of the cottage to get ready. Following the L-shaped angle of the rooms, he stripped and entered the bathroom shower. He braced his arms against the tiled wall and lifted his face to the hot spray.

She was on his mind constantly. That kiss in the squad car would unexpectedly replay itself, and his body would immediately react to the thought with a sharp tightening in his loins. Such as now. He turned the faucet from hot to cold, and growled out loud at the shock to his system.

Pulling the towel across his back, he vowed to be on his best behavior tonight. He would prove to her that they could share something meaningful, if only for a short time. There was something between them, something undeniably strong, and once they made love, he was sure she'd accept it, too.

He dressed and looked around the small bedroom in the cottage. Part of his fantasy included seeing Amanda in this room, in this bed, and he wondered what it would take to make his fantasy a reality. He felt like a teenager planning his "first time" and smiled to himself. Tonight was the test. And tomorrow...well, tomorrow would take care of itself.

But as he locked the door and headed for the car, an annoying little voice inside his head relayed an urgent warning, a warning that Vince heard but chose to ignore. He didn't need his conscience to tell him what he already knew. Like a thin, crisp, perfectly salted New York deli potato chip, one taste of Amanda Simpson would hardly be enough.

Amanda pulled back the curtain and peeked out her upstairs bedroom window. Glancing at her wrist-watch, she bit her lip. Seven-ten on Friday night, and Hester Waterbury still hadn't left for bingo. Returning to her dresser, she briskly ran a brush through her short brown curls. Strands of hair fanned out from winter static. As she patted them down with her hand, she re-alized she was shaking. She put down the brush. All she needed was for the old woman to spot Vince coming to her house to pick her up! It would be all over town by tomorrow morning.

Hearing the car door slam, she rushed to the win-dow just in time to see Hester pulling away from the house, her old station wagon chugging loudly down the street and out of sight.

"Thank God!" Amanda said out loud.

On the bed lay two dresses. She had no idea where they were going tonight, and hadn't had the nerve to call him and ask. She held up the beige cowl-neck knit dress. It was practical and businesslike, while still dressy. She draped it over her arm as she examined the royal-blue silk outfit. The two-piece dress had a V-neck jacket and a matching skirt. Two tiny pearl buttons held the jacket together in front. The outfit was beau-tiful, and she loved the way it looked on her. It was smooth, silky and soft to the touch, making her feel very feminine as it glided around her legs when she walked.

Amanda toyed with the pearl buttons, pushing them in, then out of the buttonholes. *So easy,* she thought, *he could have it off in no time at all.*

Images of her standing in front of him clad only in her flimsy pale-blue teddy flashed through her mind. He was reaching out, touching a thin satin strap, pulling it down her shoulder, first one side, then the other...

That was it. She hung up the blue silk and pulled the beige knit over her head.

She heard the doorbell ring below, and her heart turned over in her chest. Feeling like a girl on her prom, Amanda checked the mirror for any last-minute adjustments as Kimberly knocked and entered the room.

"*He's* here," she said.

"Kim..." Amanda warned. "Be nice."

"I was very polite. He's waiting in the living room. He looks funny without his uniform." Kim collapsed on the bed. "Where are you two going?"

"I don't know. I forgot to ask him." Amanda inserted an earring in her left ear. "Tell him I'll be right down, okay?"

Amanda watched Kim shuffle out of the room, refusing to dwell on her daughter's disapproval of Vince. She had other things on her mind. Such as tonight and what was going to happen.

She turned and studied her image for the last time. Her face was flushed with excitement. Oh, Lord, what was she doing? She didn't know, nor did she want to think about it right now. She finished dressing and went downstairs, greeted by the most unusual sight of her son lying on the floor between Vince's legs.

"What in the world...?"

Sean jumped up. "Mom! Guess what? The sheriff knows karate! He said he can teach me. Can I, Mom? Can I?"

Amanda took the last step and put her arm around the overexcited boy. Her gaze traveled up from the well-polished black dress shoes to the slate-gray pleated slacks, past the stylish gray-patterned jacket that complemented a stark white dress shirt and dark gray tie. He had a perfectly proportioned male body that made him seem so at home in any sort of clothing. She swallowed the breath she'd been holding and ventured forward, her eyes shifting to view his face.

He was smiling, enjoying, she knew, the obvious once-over she was giving him. His smoky gray eyes sparkled with amusement as his lips twitched in a self-mocking grin. He appeared the consummate urbanite, hand in pants pockets, a studied slouch, at ease with himself and his looks. She returned the smile, desperately trying not to ogle him.

"Karate?" she inquired.

Vince laughed. "Just one of my hidden talents." He took a step toward her and ruffled Sean's hair. "I've been kicking around the idea of offering a karate program for kids down at the firehouse. First I'd have to see what interest there was around town."

"I'll come!" Sean said. "And so would Cory. That's for sure."

"Hold on a minute," Amanda said. "Isn't he a little too young for karate?"

"Not at all," Vince said. "Many boys start younger than Sean. And don't worry, it's perfectly safe. The training involves conditioning of both body and mind. It's great discipline for boys."

"Only boys?" Kimberly interjected.

Vince turned to her. "No, of course not. Many women are experts. It's very popular for self-defense purposes. If you and your friends are interested, Kimberly, I'd be happy to run a class for your age group, too."

Kimberly shrugged. "Oh, I don't know. Doesn't seem like something I'd be needing to know here in Branchport. Nobody ever gets mugged here!"

Vince laughed. "That's true, thank God. But it's still a great sport for both men and women. Think about it. You can always let me know if there's any interest at school." He returned his attention to Sean. "In the meantime, young man, if your mother approves, I think we may start a small class in the next week or so. What do you say?"

"Oh, boy! Mom? Can I?"

Amanda smiled at her jumping son and said, "We'll see."

"That means yes, right? I'm going to call Cory right now and tell him!"

"What a dork!" Kimberly said as her brother ran up the stairs.

"Kim..." Amanda warned as she lifted her coat off the rack, "Don't start tonight, okay?"

Kim nodded. "Okay. Where are you two going, anyway?"

Amanda glanced at Vince.

"Dinner," he said. "I thought we'd go to the Steak House in town."

"No," Amanda said quickly. "Let's not go there. Let's go to Perna's. The food is great, and I haven't had Italian in ages."

"That's way up near Monticello," Kim said.

"I know," Amanda answered. "Do you mind the ride?" she asked Vince.

"No, not at all," he said as he opened the front door.

"We won't be late," Amanda said to Kim as she left.

Amanda was grateful for his unquestioning acceptance of her choice of restaurant. While the Steak House was a great place to eat, it was smack in the center of town and always crowded. She wasn't quite ready to be seen with him by the town. Too unsure of her emotions or the direction they were taking her, she felt it best to limit their exposure at this time.

She hadn't said anything to anyone about this "date." She didn't even like thinking about the evening in those terms. But then, it wasn't really a date, it was more of a fishing expedition on both their parts. It could well be that after tonight, they'd want nothing more to do with one another and whatever they were feeling would fizzle out before it even began. Why broadcast it to the whole town?

She glanced over at the man in the driver's seat. His profile was only visible through flickers of light from the highway. She studied his face, his broad shoulders, his arms, his wrist, his hand tightly gripping the steering wheel, and she felt that now-familiar glow sweep through her. It wasn't entirely his fault, she knew. This attraction was mutual, an almost living thing between them. She should be strong and ignore it, but she couldn't.

"You're very quiet," Vince said. "Want to tell me about it?"

"I was thinking about those robberies," she lied. "How's the investigation going?"

"We were able to lift a partial print from the video store, and we got lucky. The owner is an ex-con about six months out of Attica. Comes from up near Albany."

"That's good, isn't it?"

Vince nodded. "Yeah. It's the first break we've had. Sam is upstate now trying to check him out. There's definitely more than one involved, and they're staying nearby. I can feel it."

"Have there been any more robberies?"

"None in the past week, but with the weekend here, I won't be surprised if they try again."

"So you'll be working all weekend again?" she asked.

Vince glanced her way and grinned. "Want to keep me company on a stakeout? We could neck in the squad car."

Amanda laughed. "You're impossible. Slow down, Sheriff."

"If I go any slower, Amanda—"

"Not you! The car." She pointed out the windshield. "The restaurant is up ahead on the right."

A bright red-and-white neon sign flashed on the otherwise pitch-black road. Vince turned the car onto the gravel parking lot and cut the engine. He sat silently contemplating the steering wheel for a moment before turning his full gaze to her.

He reached over and stroked her cheek with his index finger. "Hungry?"

She nodded her answer. His touch lingered after his hand disappeared. It marked her, warmed her, cleansed her. She was hungry all right. She was starved.

The main dining area of the restaurant was small, intimate and dimly lit. The tables were round with the typical red-and-white checkered cloths covering each one. Half were occupied with patrons, but no one glanced their way as a waiter escorted them to a table in the corner. A dark green wine bottle encased in straw held a partially melted candle. After seating Amanda, the waiter struck a match and lit the remaining stub, casting a warm, welcoming glow.

Opening the menu, Vince let out a low but appreciative whistle.

"This is some selection!" he said.

"What did you expect?" she asked.

He had the good grace to look embarrassed. "I guess I'm more of a city snob than I thought." He looked over her head and observed the room. "This room reminds me of a little favorite of mine on Bleeker Street in New York. You don't get this kind of atmosphere in any of the newer restaurants anymore. Cozy. I like it."

"I thought you would," she said. "And maybe you missed some of mom's home cooking?" she teased.

Vince laughed. "How I wish! Unfortunately my mother is not the world's best cook, Italian or otherwise. When I was a kid, my grandmother would send pasta over once a week to be sure we had one good meal! She's gone now, and my father bought my mother a microwave two years ago. That was it. She doesn't even *pretend* to cook anymore!"

"Do you have a big family?"

"Only an older sister. She's married, with a couple of kids. But I have a multitude of cousins. There was a time, when I was a kid, that I could walk down the street where I lived and meet only relatives. It was a great way to grow up."

They placed their order and requested a bottle of Valpolicella. The waiter returned with it promptly and filled the small glasses with the dark red liquid. They toasted, and Amanda took a sip. It was hearty and dry with a fruity taste that warmed her insides.

"Why did you come to Branchport?"

She watched his face grow somber in response to her question. He sat back in the wooden chair and looked away from her for a moment before capturing her eyes with a compelling stare that seemed chock-full of emotion, yet his answer was only one word.

"Peace."

Amanda was jarred. It was always the first word that came to mind when she thought about her hometown.

"Is that all you're going to say?" she asked.

"I don't know how much more you want to hear."

"All of it."

Vince returned a halfhearted smile. "I don't think you'd like all of it. Some, maybe—" he shook his head "—but definitely not all."

Amanda leaned forward and put her elbows on the table and rested her chin in her palms. "Tell me," she urged.

Vince stared at the woman so near, yet in many ways so far away from him. He remembered her reaction to his gun and had no doubt about how she would react if he blurted out that he'd killed a fifteen-year-old boy. He didn't want to see the shock on her face, the disgust he himself still battled in his mind. He shook his head again.

"It's a long story."

"I'm not going anywhere. Tell me. Please, Vince."

His heart skipped a short beat at the sound of his name on her lips.

"I've been a cop all my adult life. My father was a cop, my uncle and at least half of my cousins." He grinned. "It became a family tradition, you see. For almost twenty years I worked some of the roughest neighborhoods in the city. I did eight years in the South Bronx alone."

"Not exactly pleasant work?"

"You could say that. Anyway, I'm not complaining. I loved every minute of it. I used to thrive on the tension of the streets. The adrenaline pumped and kept you alert, on the edge. It was great, until . . ."

"Until?"

He took a deep breath. "Until two years ago. My partner was killed in a robbery attempt." He shook his head. "It was bad, real bad."

She watched that faraway look return once again and knew instinctively that he was reliving some private horror of which she might never truly know or understand.

"I'm sorry," she said.

Her soft words broke into his reverie. "It's over," he said abruptly. "Tell me about you."

Amanda shrugged. "There really isn't much to tell. You've been in Branchport several weeks now. You probably know all there is to know already."

"What do you mean?"

Amanda laughed. "Surely that infamous grapevine you mentioned hasn't neglected to supply the story of the fall of Amanda Simpson? It's still a favorite topic of conversation, even after all these years."

"You mean about you and your husband having to get married? Besides being, what, fifteen years ago? It's hardly a big deal anymore. Most celebrities you read about are pregnant before they marry anyway."

"I'm sure it's no big deal in L.A. or New York, but in Branchport, they still embroider scarlet letters for such offenses."

Vince sat back and took a sip of wine. The candle-light flickered across her face as they stared at each other.

"Did you love him?" he asked softly, silently wondering why he did.

Amanda toyed with the stem of her glass and looked away from his intent gaze. "I thought I did. Back then. But things look different than they really are when you're in high school."

"He hurt you."

"Yes. He did. But in a lot of ways, it was as much my fault as his. Billy never grew up, but I did. The things that were such fun at seventeen were the very things that caused us problems after we were married and had the children." She managed a wry smile. "He has a very hard time with responsibility. He's always been looking to grab that golden ring, the one that was going to make him rich and happy. He never realized that happiness has to come from inside, not out."

"And you're happy now?"

She took a deep breath and let it out audibly. "Yes, I am. I'm happy with my children and my work, and my life here in Branchport. It wasn't until we moved around so much that I came to appreciate all I had right here growing up. I want that life for my children."

"And you plan to stay."

She studied him for a moment. "Yes," she said softly but emphatically. "I plan to stay."

Dinner conversation provided Amanda with information about his divorce and his daughter who now lived in Florida. He talked at length about her, showing a side of himself she hadn't thought existed.

Amanda had to smile when he related some incidents he'd lived through with his Chrissy. From his description, she could see the girl clearly. She and Kimberly seemed much alike. She was sure now that Kimberly reminded him of his own daughter.

It seemed strange picturing Vince as a family man. He was too self-assured, too much the loner—a typical, city bachelor. The realization that he was both made him all the more appealing. Yet part of Amanda couldn't dream of a more deadly or dangerous combination in a man.

They rode home in companionable silence. Vince held her hand, and she let him. She was comfortable with the company and mellow from the wine. Earlier reservations gone, she had to admit it was one of the best nights she'd ever spent in her life. As his Corvette pulled into her driveway, she acknowledged that she didn't want it to end.

Vince brought her hand to his mouth and kissed her fingertips as he stared into her eyes.

"Would you like some coffee?" she asked softly.

He didn't want coffee, but he didn't want to leave, either. He nodded. "I'd love some."

Amanda glanced across the street at the darkened windows of the Waterbury residence as she unlocked her front door. Nothing stirred. She was annoyed at herself for even caring, but old habits were hard to break. She forced herself to put it out of her mind.

Amanda beckoned Vince to follow her into the kitchen where she filled the coffeepot.

"Mugs are in the cabinet to the right above the sink. I'm just going up to check on the kids. I'll be right back."

"Take your time," Vince said.

Amanda tiptoed into Sean's room and covered the snoring boy who lay sprawled on his back diagonally across the bed. She smiled as she smoothed his hair from his brow.

A light flickered through the crack in the door of Kim's room.

"Kim?" Amanda called softly.

She opened the door and saw the small television on in the corner of the room. Kimberly was sleeping soundly, clutching a small, worn, brown teddy bear that she still kept in her room from when she was just a baby. Sean made fun of her, and Kim swore she only kept the stuffed animal for sentimental reasons; but a night didn't go by without that bear finding its way into bed with the teenager.

Amanda clicked off the television set and crept silently out of the room. She stopped at the foot of the stairs and hugged the wooden post as she observed Vince in the living room arranging two mugs, milk and sugar on the coffee table. She watched this display of domesticity with a discreet smile on her face.

Vince looked up at her. "I hope you don't mind," he said as he gestured toward the table.

Amanda smiled. "Not at all. I like being served."

"Everything okay?" he asked.

She walked toward him and accepted the steaming cup. "They're both fine. Sleeping like logs." She sat in the love seat across from him. "You know, I realize they're getting older, more independent, but seeing them asleep always makes them seem like such babies to me.''

"I know," he said.

"You miss Chrissy, don't you?"

"All the time," he answered. "It never really goes away. I thought I'd go crazy when Linda first took her away. The house was like a morgue. I hated to go home at night." He took a quick sip of the hot liquid. "I guess that was when I got involved in PAL."

"PAL?"

"Police Athletic League. It's a place city kids can go to learn about sports instead of drugs. We don't make it with all of them, but when you click with a street kid, it's very satisfying. It filled a void for me."

"And now, you miss that, too."

"Yes, I hope these karate classes work out."

"Well, if Sean's enthusiasm is any indication, I'd say you'll have a full house for your first class."

"Then you'll let him take the course?"

"Well . . ." Amanda hesitated.

"You have some reservations about this, don't you? It's perfectly safe if properly taught. Trust me. I know what I'm doing."

Amanda leaned back on the sofa. *Trust* was a good word to use, she decided. She trusted him with Sean's safety, but there were other considerations, ones she wasn't as easy about.

"What is it, Amanda? What's bothering you?"

"This sort of thing takes a long time to learn, doesn't it?"

"There are many types of martial arts, but, yes, all take years to master."

"Well . . . I guess it's just that I don't want Sean becoming involved in something, becoming obsessed with it—as he tends to do with things—and then have to abandon it."

"Why would he have to abandon it? The program will go on and progress along with him."

"As long as *you're* here."

Vince stared at her in silence, his face a mask. With an almost imperceptible shake of his head, he said, "There are others who could pick up where I left off."

Amanda arched her brows in speculation. "Like who?"

"Karate schools in the area. I could check into it if you'd like," he said.

"Perhaps you should. Or give it some more thought before you involve a lot of youngsters in something you won't be able to finish."

"You're really hung up on finishing things, aren't you, Amanda?"

Vince stood. She could tell he was agitated by the turn the conversation was taking, but she refused to back down.

"Maybe I am."

"Maybe you should learn to live for the moment."

He pulled her up to stand in front of him, then bent his head to hers and kissed her. It was a light kiss, a gentle caress, a brush of one pair of lips upon another; but to Amanda's heightened senses, it fractured reality and made the room spin. She reached up and grabbed hold of his forearms for support.

Vince pulled her closer, deepening the kiss as he opened her mouth with his tongue and explored inside. She joined him, tasting the coffee, feeling his heat. Suddenly she was warm, wet, weak.

One part of her brain wanted to do as he said, to only live for the moment, but another part, the more vulnerable, insecure one, couldn't handle it. She wanted more, so much more than he could give.

It wasn't only her own stability that was at stake, she rationalized. She had two children that were her sole responsibility. No, better not to give in so easily. Better to be alone. Better to be safe.

She pushed him away, and he released her.

His pupils were dilated, exposing only a smoky gray ring around the stark black gaze.

Vince's arms encircled her waist. Each hand ascended slowly up her sides, stopping just below her breasts. His large hands spanned her rib cage as his thumbs simultaneously grazed her nipples. Together they watched in fascination as his fingers rubbed back and forth, back and forth, making the sensitive peaks taut and hard as pebbles. Amanda closed her eyes at the sensations he was arousing.

"I want you, Amanda," he whispered. She opened her eyes to stare back again into his. "And you want me." He shook his head slightly. "This isn't going to go away." He touched her lips with his own. "I'm not going to let it."

Vince cupped her face in his hands before capturing her mouth once again. He kissed her thoroughly, completely, staking a claim, marking his territory. When he let her go, she fell against him.

Holding her by the shoulders, he gently pushed her down onto the sofa.

"I'll call you," he said as he picked up his jacket and walked out.

Amanda stared at the front door, too stunned to move, too confused to try. For what would she do if she did indeed catch up with him? Slap his face? Or pull him back inside?

Glancing down at her fully aroused breasts, she placed both her hands over her stomach in an attempt to control the tremors.

She was afraid she knew all too well what the answer would be.

Six

What are you wearing Saturday night?" Polly asked.

Amanda cradled the phone securely between her ear and shoulder as she plopped six hot dogs into a pot of boiling water.

"I don't know, Polly. Probably the blue silk two-piece. It's the best outfit I have, and I'm not about to buy something new for a party at Liddy Halverson's."

"Can you believe Sam is thirty-five already? God, I remember when he was shorter than me," Polly said.

"He's still shorter than you."

Polly laughed. "Yeah, he is. Anyway, it'll be fun. Liddy said he doesn't expect a thing, so it should really be a big surprise."

Amanda emptied an entire box of shell macaroni into a second pot of boiling water and stirred. *Another gourmet dinner,* she thought.

"Do you want John and me to give you a lift over?"

"No, I'll drive myself. This way I can leave early."

"Why are you planning to leave early? I thought the kids were spending the night with friends."

"They are, but I can only take Liddy Halverson for just so long. Then I lose it."

Polly laughed. "Well, maybe this time you'll change your mind. I hear she invited the sheriff."

Amanda shifted the phone to the other ear. "Vince is going?"

"So I hear. Why not ask him to pick you up?"

"Definitely not."

"Amanda—"

"Don't start, Polly." She tested a piece of macaroni. "I haven't changed my mind."

"Suit yourself," Polly said. "But I still think you're crazy."

"See you Saturday."

Amanda hung up the phone as the children walked into the kitchen. She grabbed two terry-cloth holders, lifted the hot pot off the stove and drained the macaroni in the colander.

"What's for dinner?" Sean asked.

"Hot dogs and macaroni and cheese. And maybe a salad, if the lettuce isn't brown," Amanda answered.

"Yum," said Sean.

"Ick," said Kimberly.

Amanda spooned a helping of margarine into the macaroni and emptied the packet of freeze-dried cheese into the pot.

"I'm sorry, Kimberly. I know you hate this, but I never made it to the supermarket today, so it'll have to do."

"I'm not hungry anyway," the teenager replied.

Amanda heard the petulance in her daughter's voice, but she refused to rise to the bait.

"Did you finish folding the laundry?" Amanda asked Kim.

"Yes. I'll put it away after dinner."

"Sean can help you."

"Aw, Mom!"

"Don't 'aw, Mom' me, young man. Just do it," she said as she spooned out the macaroni.

Some days it was more difficult than others to be captain as well as chief petty officer, and today was one of them. Her hard-won "freedom" was less than appealing when the burden of parenting fell entirely on her shoulders. Sometimes she longed for that mythical knight in shining armor to sweep her off her feet and take her away from all this.

Funny, how lately that knight had visited her dreams more often. Funny, how he wore a uniform with a shiny tin star that almost matched the slate gray of his eyes. As she ate dinner her mind wandered to the feel of his fingers brushing across her breasts. She forcibly pushed the thought out of her mind as she'd repeatedly done since that night.

"How was school today?" she asked.

"I had to cut open a frog in biology. When I put the knife in, all this gunk squirted out. It got all over my red sweatshirt and smelled so bad I thought I was going to throw up—"

"Can we change the subject during dinner, Kimberly?"

"Well, I just wanted to know if you think it'll wash. I love that sweatshirt!"

"I'm sure it will." Amanda pierced another hot dog with her fork and brought it to her plate. "How is Tommy?" she asked without looking at her daughter.

"He's okay, I guess."

"You guess?"

"I haven't seen him too much. You *did* tell me not to, didn't you?"

"Yes, but I assumed you would still see him and talk to him in school."

"We talk. He told me his parents went to speak to the sheriff last week."

"Last week? Why did it take them so long?"

"They were both out of town. They both have these real important jobs and they travel a lot. I don't think they even care about Tommy."

"I can't believe that, Kim. They're probably just busy."

"Yeah, too busy for their own kid. He's real lonely, you know, Mom? He's a nice guy, and I feel sorry for him." Kim looked at her. "Can't I at least invite him over here to do homework sometime? He's not bad, honest, Mom."

Amanda looked at her daughter and sighed. Ever since she was a little girl, Kim had had a soft heart. Always picked up strays—cats, dogs, an occasional wounded bird. She never could force herself to refuse to help Kim take care of them, either.

"Sure," she said and patted Kim's arm. "He can come here for homework. But only when I'm home. Deal?"

Kim smiled. "Deal."

"And how about you, Sean. How was your day?"

"Pretty okay. I have a paper for you to sign about the karate class. Sheriff Messina's a pretty neat guy, you know, Mom? He said he'd start real soon, and he did. I can do it, right, Mom? Me and Cory can't wait!''

"Cory and I," Amanda corrected. "If you really want to, you may. But remember, the sheriff is only going to be here until Odus Tucker is better, so you may not be able to finish the program.''

"I know.''

"I know you know, Sean, but I don't want you to be disappointed when it ends.''

"Maybe the sheriff will like Branchport so much by then that he'll stay. Wouldn't that be great, Mom?''

Amanda's heart skipped a beat at the thought. "Don't count on it," she said softly, more to herself than to Sean. "When are the classes starting?''

"Next Tuesday. Hiii-ya!'' he screamed and savagely cut the air with his right hand.

Amanda grabbed her son's wrist and placed it back on the table. "Save it for karate class, please.''

Kimberly began to clear away the dishes as Amanda filled the teapot with water. The hour after dinner was her own private time. When the kitchen was cleaned, Amanda poured herself a cup of tea.

She took a deep breath and relaxed. Thoughts of the Halverson party entered her mind. She hadn't seen Vince since their dinner date. He hadn't called though he'd said he would. Maybe he'd thought better of it. Amanda told herself it was for the best, but she couldn't help feeling sick inside even if she did get exactly what she'd asked for.

Amanda toyed with the idea of not going Saturday night, but she'd just be avoiding the inevitable. It was impossible to not see him for the remainder of his stay in Branchport. Sooner or later they'd meet, and Liddy's party was as good a place as any, she supposed.

She rose and dumped the remaining tea down the drain, placing her empty cup in the dishwasher. She told herself it didn't matter, and tried to put it out of her mind. But she couldn't. He was becoming an obsession with her. She fantasized all the time, day and night, of what it would be like to make love with him, while opposing feelings of dread and longing battled inside her head.

She set the wash dial for a full load and leaned against the vibrating machine.

He was right. It wouldn't just go away.

"Surprise!"

Everyone screamed as Sam Halverson entered the decorated basement. Liddy was all over him in a minute, kissing his face and wrapping both arms around his middle, while everyone else gathered around to offer their congratulations.

Amanda discreetly looked over Sam's shoulder, but Vince wasn't with him. As the night wore on she made her way around the room waiting for someone to say something about the sheriff, but no one did. She didn't dare ask anyone if he was coming, but she couldn't keep her eyes from frequently darting to the door.

"Looking for someone?"

Amanda turned to face her brother. "Oh, John. No, of course not. Where's Polly?"

"Over there in the corner talking her head off." He lifted his glass. "Can I get you a refill?"

"No thanks. I'm nursing the punch."

"Liddy's secret recipe? That stuff's so weak, it tastes like fruit juice."

"It's good enough for..."

Amanda stopped talking as Liddy escorted Vince into the room, introducing him to people he hadn't yet met. She watched as he scanned the room and homed in on her. The intensity of his gaze caused her stomach to churn. Turning away, she faced a smirking John.

"Don't be so obvious, Amanda," he said.

"I don't know what you're talking about."

"If you're so hung up on the guy, why don't you go out with him?"

"I'll tell you the same thing I told Polly—I'm not interested."

John smiled and shook his head. "You never could lie very well."

"Hello."

A wave of pure pleasure basted her from head to toe at the sound of his voice.

"Hi, Vince. How are you?" John put out his hand, and the two men shook.

"Fine, John. How's business?"

Amanda stood by as they discussed the finer points of hardware. He barely acknowledged her presence, seeming perfectly at ease and content to swap small talk with her brother.

She on the other hand, wanted to scream. She wanted to turn around and walk away and stop pretending that she didn't care. She also wanted to touch him, run her fingers through his hair and nibble on that pouting lower lip until she'd had her fill.

"Sheriff! I'm glad you're here," Mike Powell interrupted. "I've been meaning to ask you how the investigation on the robberies is going?"

Vince made room for the mayor in their little group. "Actually, it's moving along. We have some solid leads up in the lake district we're working on," he said non-committally.

"There are a lot of vacant houses up there this time of year. That could take forever."

"We'll do our best," Vince said.

Mike slapped him on the back. "I've no doubt of that, Sheriff!"

Amanda tuned them out as she spotted Polly dancing a Lindy with one of the other women across the room. Thinking it safer to join her sister-in-law, she began to ease herself away from the men. She took one step and felt a strong grip on her hand. Vince entwined her fingers with his, firmly holding her in place. She looked up at him as he continued to speak with the mayor and her brother. A chill ran up her spine as his thumb lightly drew whorls on her sensitive palm. She was hardly aware that the conversation ended and they were alone until he turned to her.

"Hi," he said softly.

"H-hi."

"You look beautiful tonight."

Amanda put her head down. "Thank you."

Vince lifted her chin and held her face in place as he examined each of her features one by one.

"I missed you," he said.

"Vince—"

"Tell me the truth. Just this once. Didn't you miss me, too, even a little?"

She looked into his fathomless gray eyes and couldn't lie. "Yes."

Her body swayed toward his, and he moved into it until they touched. The music changed from fast to slow, and he pulled her toward the dance area. She followed, welcoming any excuse to be in his arms.

Without a word, they wrapped their arms around each other and she rested her head on his chest. The steady rhythm of his heartbeat soothed her, made her feel safe, secure, at home.

Vince tucked her body into his and held her tightly. They fit together as perfectly as two pieces of a puzzle. She was soft and warm, and his body was on fire for her. He closed his eyes as they barely moved to the music. It wasn't getting any better; if anything, it was getting worse by the day.

He ached for her, morning, noon and night. He hadn't called, thinking that maybe she was right: if he broke contact with her, he'd get over it. But his thoughts and feelings intensified. And it wasn't just physical—though Lord only knew how long he could go on without having her. He wanted to be *with* her, listen to her talk, hear her laugh, see her smile, watch her just be . . . Amanda.

"I didn't think you were coming," she said.

"I wasn't. With Sam having the night off, I was planning to work till midnight. But one of the other deputies took my place." He grinned. "I think they wanted me out of their hair."

Amanda lifted her eyebrows. "Making changes down at the station?"

"Some."

Her palm moved to his shoulder, and she felt the bulge from his gun. She pulled her hand away. "I wouldn't think you'd need this here, tonight," she said.

"There may be one or two dangerous characters around," he teased as he brought the same hand to his lips and kissed her palm. His eyes grew stormy, and her heart skipped a beat. "You never can tell . . ."

The music stopped, and Liddy announced it was time to cut the cake and open the gifts. Amanda found herself paying more attention to Vince than Sam's gifts. Once again, his mere presence threw her emotions off kilter. Did she want him, or didn't she? She was supposed to be a mature woman who knew her own mind. If that was so, why couldn't she make it up?

Amanda excused herself, picked up her purse and headed for the bathroom. She splashed cold water on her hands and wrists and examined her image in the mirror. The face looking back at her was that of a woman she didn't want to acknowledge. She was feeling too much, caring too much, and all that emotion was clearly visible. She didn't want to feel this way about any man, and certainly not Vince Messina.

The dancing was over when she re-entered the room. Vince was in the corner talking to a group that included Liddy and Sam. Amanda halted in her tracks. Suddenly she had no desire to go back in there and join in. She was restless, and agitated, but she didn't know why. She only knew she wanted to get away from here.

Spotting John near the bar, she made her way over to her brother.

"I'm leaving," she said.

"Already?"

"I've had about enough. Tell Polly I'll call her tomorrow. Say good-night for me, okay?"

He kissed her cheek. "Okay. I'll stop by tomorrow."

"Not too early. The kids are staying with friends. I'm going to sleep in for a change."

Vince saw Amanda grab her coat and head for the door. He'd been watching her every movement since she'd disappeared from his side. He checked his watch. Why was she leaving? Was something wrong?

He excused himself and followed her out the door. The late winter night was sharp and brisk, and he felt the bite of the cold air. His footsteps made a crunching sound against the stone driveway as he came up behind her.

"Amanda?"

Car keys in hand, Amanda turned. "Yes?"

"Something wrong?"

"No."

"Then why are you leaving?"

"I'm tired."

"All of a sudden?"

"All of a sudden."

Amanda inserted the key into the car door. Vince took hold of her shoulders and turned her to him.

"I don't believe you."

"I don't care what you believe."

"Don't do this, Amanda. Don't build that wall up again. I've waited all week for tonight. To see you, talk to you. And now, you walk out without a word."

Amanda sighed and fell back against her car. "Why won't you leave me alone?"

Vince leaned over her, his arms pinning her to the cold metal frame. "Because I can't . . ."

His lips covered hers in a hungry, devouring kiss. She opened her mouth for him, and his tongue accepted the invitation to plunder the sweet secrets within. A moan caught in her throat as the reality of the moment picked her up and spun her around. He was here, now, touching her, wanting her . . . and God help her, there was nowhere else on earth she'd rather be.

He opened her coat and moved his hands over her back and her waist, coming to rest on her buttocks. He cupped her against him. He was on fire as he pressed himself into the cradle of her hips.

A responding jolt of desire rocked through her. Amanda's hands reached across his back and massaged the tense muscles as his mouth moved down her neck to her collarbone and back up to nuzzle her ear.

"Come home with me—"

"Evenin'."

Vince's head popped up and Amanda blinked rapidly to clear her vision as the intruding voice broke through the cloud of passion.

"M-Mr. Walters? Hello," Amanda said.

Vince nodded at the man walking his dog down the street.

"A bit cool, isn't it?" Mr. Walters continued. "Shouldn't be out here without a coat on, young man. Flu's real bad this year."

Vince nodded again, unable to find his voice. A coat was the last thing he needed. His skin was burning hot, and his blood was pumping at record speed.

"Well, good night, now." The man continued on his way, leaving the bewildered couple to stare after him.

Amanda rebuttoned her coat and opened her car door. Vince stopped her with a hand on her arm.

"I meant it, Amanda. Come home with me."

She was angry as well as embarrassed. She'd allowed it to happen again. Once again, her nonexistent willpower proved to be her undoing. She had to get away from him.

"Once and for all, Sheriff, leave me alone."

"You weren't exactly pushing me away a minute ago. Why don't you admit it, Amanda? You don't know what you want. It's not me you're mad at. It's your-self.''

She slipped into the car, but he stopped her from shutting the door.

"If you're so desperate for a willing bedmate to-night, Sheriff, I suggest you go back inside and look around. I'm sure someone will be happy to accom-modate you."

Vince's jaw tightened, and he stepped back from the car. "Maybe I will, Mrs. Simpson. Maybe I will."

He slammed the car door and walked away.

Seven

Amanda was restless. A glance at the clock told her it wasn't eleven yet. Eleven o'clock on a Saturday night and here she sat alone in her kitchen. She had only spited herself by leaving the party early. She toyed with the button on her two-piece blue silk dress and pondered her fate. All dressed up and nowhere to go.

She poured a glass of white wine from a bottle that had been hidden in back of the refrigerator. She didn't even know what kind it was, as the label was long gone. After taking a sip, she swished the liquid around in her mouth and decided it wasn't all that bad. She carried the glass into the living room and snapped on a table lamp before sitting on the sofa.

The television remote control was on the coffee table, and she punched the power button then flicked around the channels. A romantic romp from the Thirties materialized on the screen. The well-known actors

of the past bantered back and forth and she forced
herself to sit back to enjoy the movie. During the
commercial break, she refilled her wineglass and returned to the sofa. But the more she stared at the
screen, the more blurred it became. Instead of the actors, she saw herself and Vince, huddled against her car
in front of Liddy's house. His breath was warm on her
face, his mouth commanding, his kiss persuading. . . .

At some point she lost interest in the movie and
dozed. She blinked awake and stared at the snowy TV
screen. The wineglass in front of her was empty, and
she was sprawled out on the sofa. Slowly she sat up and
turned off the set. The house was so quiet, so empty, a
chill ran down her back. She couldn't remember the
last time she was completely alone at home. One child
or the other was always with her.

Amanda rose and entered the kitchen. It was one in
the morning. She supposed she should change and go
to bed, but she wasn't the least bit tired anymore. The
nap seemed to refresh her. Aimlessly she roamed the
house touching the furniture, checking the front door,
passing her solitary reflection in the hallway mirror. A
high flush brightened her cheeks, whether from the
wine or the direction her thoughts were taking, she
didn't dare decide.

The idea sneaked and then steamrolled into her
mind. Once there, she couldn't stop it. *I wonder if he's
still at Liddy's?*

It didn't matter, she told herself. It was none of her
business where he spent the night. But her stomach
churned at the thought that he was anywhere but
home—alone. Something, somewhere deep inside her
had to know for sure.

She could call Liddy, she supposed, just to say thanks, but she wouldn't give the woman the satisfaction of her curiosity. Amanda glanced out the front window. The street was quiet, serenely wrapped in darkness. Hester's blinds were firmly in place. One streetlamp was burnt out, and the area around it was pitch black. As her eyes passed over her car in the driveway, its headlights, hood and grill formed a mocking face to her overactive imagination. It seemed to call out to her... *Come on, Amanda, a quick ride, that's all it would take to know....*

Heart pounding with excitement as well as fear, she backed away from the window. Amanda brought a shaky palm up to her chest and took a deep breath. Could she do it? She shook her head. How juvenile to check up on him. Why, it was something Kim and her friends would do, not a grown woman in her thirties with two children.

But the image of him alone, at home, sleeping in bed, possibly dreaming about her and what they could be doing together was frighteningly real and very tempting. Just a quick ride, she thought. Who would know? Amanda picked up her coat and keys and almost raced out the door before she lost her nerve. She'd only pass his house just to be sure he was home. What harm could that do?

The old Gates's fishing cabin, Polly had said. She knew where it was. When she and John were children, they used to fish up at the lake for hours on end. Their father would drive them up to the dock and drop them off early in the morning. Mom would pack a lunch, and they'd stay until midafternoon, baiting their hooks with rolled pieces of soft, doughy white bread, catching sunnies and shiners along with an occasional perch.

It had been great fun and always a treat to go. She felt an excitement of a different kind this time as the treat she thought of was tall, two-legged and decidedly male.

She made the turn onto the north side of town and followed the rutted dirt road up to the end. There it was. The cabin was set back off the road, a hodge-podge house that had begun its life as one room and had been reincarnated time and again until each additional room formed a new angle. Strange as it looked, the house had a homey appearance. Amanda pulled up in front of the long gravel driveway and stopped. The black Corvette was parked way up near the front door.

So, he was home. But was he alone? It's none of your business, she repeated to herself over and over in a self-admonishing litany.

Go home, Amanda.

A pale light flickered through the front bay window. He was still up: the television was on. At the thought, tightness gripped and twisted her insides. Vince was here, right now, only a few feet away from her. And she had all night.

She wasn't a fool. She knew what would happen if she knocked at his door in the middle of the night. Amanda's heart began to pound anew. What if he was still angry? What if he turned her away? Her hands clenched and unclenched the steering wheel, and she began to perspire in the cold night air.

All she would have to do is knock on the door. She pictured his surprise. He'd take her in his arms, kiss her, then take her to his bed. They'd make beautiful, slow love all night....

She squeezed her eyes closed. Just once, she thought. Just this once, and then they'd both be satisfied. It wasn't a lot to ask, was it? It had been such a long time. And she wanted him so.

Amanda opened the car door and took one of the biggest steps of her life.

Vince dropped his pants and stepped out of them. The air in the bedroom was cold, but it felt good to his overheated body. He was still tied up in knots over the events of the evening. He'd stayed at the party until it ended just to prove he could have a good time without Amanda. That he had a miserable one added to his sour mood.

He couldn't get her out of his head, no matter how hard he tried. God, she could rile him! She was driving him crazy, running hot as could be one minute, and cold as ice the next. *His* body temperature couldn't cope with her mercurial changes, but he couldn't do a damn thing about it.

Except leave. Now that's a thought, he told himself as he stepped into the shower and turned the water on full blast. Get the hell out of this godforsaken town while he still had half a mind. He nodded as the water hit him full in the face. That's what he'd do. Monday morning first thing, he'd go see Odus at the convalescence center to see how he was doing. He could take a couple more weeks, if need be, but it was becoming increasingly obvious that Branchport was not for him. He needed people, congestion—action! Then maybe this woman would disappear from his mind. That was it. Six months back in the Bronx, he wouldn't even remember her face.

He turned off the tap and covered his head with the towel as he rubbed his hair dry. Slowly he pulled the terry cloth down across each feature. Her face. Amanda's face. There it was again, crystal clear in his mind's eye: her eyes closed, her lips soft, her mouth open, waiting for his kiss...

Vince cocked his head. A sound came from the other room. Had he locked the door? He didn't remember. He was getting as bad as the locals leaving doors unlocked, windows open. Wrapping the towel around his middle, he moved slowly toward his revolver, lifting it gently, soundlessly, from its holster. He listened intently, but heard only the low droning of the TV he'd left on in the living room.

Then he heard a shuffle of footsteps. Someone was out there. He leaned his body against the wall and peered through the opened doorway. No one. The thieves were still at large, but would they be so bold to try to rob the sheriff's house when he was home? Maybe they didn't know he was the sheriff. The cabin was appealingly isolated and at the end of a dead-end road.

He placed one bare foot in front of the other and silently inched his way along the living room wall toward the hallway where he'd heard the noise. Turning quickly, he saw a form in the dim, almost nonexistent light, and his reflexes took over.

In one lightning motion, he had the perpetrator plastered to the wall, his forearm wedged against a throat and his .38 pointed at the intruder's head.

"Vince?"

Before the raspy sound of his name even registered in his mind, the soft body and distinctive perfume penetrated his senses. As if in slow motion, he dropped his arm from her neck and the gun from her temple. Catching his breath, he leaned both elbows on the wall above her head, effectively pinning her in place. As the tension eased from his body, another more urgent need took its place.

"God...Amanda..."

His head swooped down, and his mouth captured hers in a hot, wet, devouring kiss. The taste of fear in his mouth was replaced with the sweet flavor of wine and woman. His tongue touched hers lightly, and a bolt of pure pleasure shot through his body as she reciprocated, opening her mouth and twisting her head to gain better access to him. Like a spark to dry wood, his body caught fire, fueling an uncontrollable arousal. He felt himself swell against the terry-cloth towel as he pressed into her soft body.

Amanda whimpered into his mouth as myriad sensations assaulted her from all directions. He was consuming her whole, making her dizzy, spinning her fragile emotions totally out of control. She reached up and splayed her fingers across his back, massaging droplets of water into his skin as she kneaded the firm muscles.

His lips left hers to map a trail of moist, opened-mouth kisses down her neck and collarbone and up again. Her knees became weak as his breath reached her ear, and she felt herself sliding. The wall and her rubbery legs could no longer support her.

"Vince...please...Vince..."

His name floated over him like a caress as his mouth found hers once more. Arms trembling, he slowly moved his lips from hers and gently kissed each cheek, each eye, before coming to rest on the middle of her forehead.

Vince looked down at the woman before him. "You scared the hell out of me."

Amanda placed her hands on his shoulders. "*I* scared *you*?"

Vince moved back. They both looked at the gun in his hand.

"Yeah." He smiled. "I see what you mean." Taking her hand, he led her into the brighter living room.

"I knocked," she said. "But no one answered. The door was open and I called—"

"I was in the shower."

Amanda suddenly realized what he was wearing. She looked away from his blatantly aroused body and stared at the blank corner of the ceiling.

Seeing her discomfort, but not being able to do a damn thing about it, Vince cupped her chin in his hand and forced her to face him.

"Why are you here?" he asked softly.

"I—I wasn't tired and went for a ride and your light was—"

Vince's eyes were stormy gray and intense. "The time for fun and games is over, Amanda."

She swallowed what seemed like a rock the size of an orange. The tip of her tongue peeked out of her mouth and licked her lower lip.

"Tell me . . ." he urged. "The truth."

Amanda shook her head, unable to vocalize what was in her heart, in her head and pounding in her body. She reached out a hand and touched the soft hair on his chest, running her fingers through it as she moved closer to him.

"You," she said so softly he had to strain to hear her. "I came for you."

His breathing caused his chest to heave as he inhaled and placed his large hand over her smaller one. Lifting it to his mouth, he kissed her palm, licking its

center before bringing it up to the side of his face and
holding it in place. He shut his eyes for an instant as if
to savor the moment, and his nostrils expanded with a
rush of air as his features became taut with desire.

As he opened his eyes their gazes met in a passion-
ate embrace. "Thank God," he whispered, then drew
her with him as he walked backward toward the doorway of his bedroom.

Amanda followed willingly, overwhelmed by the
meekness that invaded her system now that she'd admitted her need to him. She stood in the middle of his
bedroom and watched as he pushed the revolver back
into the holster on the dresser.

Vince sat down on the edge of the bed and beckoned her forward. Slowly, Amanda walked to him. He
took hold of her hands and pulled her to stand between his legs. Reaching up, he grabbed the lapels of
her coat in each hand and pulled them down over her
shoulders, effectively trapping her arms. He nuzzled
her breasts through the material of her silk dress, wetting the fabric with the heat of his mouth.

The coat dropped to the floor as he released it. His
fingers toyed briefly with the two tiny pearl buttons on
her top. Then, as she had imagined, Amanda watched
him easily slip them through the fastenings and push
back the material to view what laid beneath. He ran his
fingers up the front of her belly to the mounds of her
breasts, the slinky material of her undergarments sen-
suously skimming across her skin. She felt her nipples
pucker from the friction.

He removed the remainder of her outfit until she
stood before him clad only in a baby blue satin teddy.
One thin strap fell from her shoulder inviting Vince to
pull down the other, which he wasted no time in doing.

Her high, firm breasts stopped the descent, and the blue satin hung precariously across the twin peaks, baring only a glimpse of the dark pink tops of her nipples.

Vince leaned back on his outstretched arms and drank in the sight of her. His gaze meandered from the delicate mound outlined through the thin teddy up to her round belly, higher to the glory of her upturned breasts, to her face, soft, languorous and ready for love.

"You are beautiful," he whispered. "And I want you so very much, I don't believe you're really here."

Amanda leaned forward and placed her hands on his shoulders. "I'm really here. For you, Vince." She rubbed her hands across his chest, threading her fingers through the mat of thick hair. "Touch me, please . . . all over. . . ."

He pulled her down to him, and they lay face-to-face sprawled diagonally across the rumpled double bed. Vince tugged on the teddy, and it fell forward exposing the tight buds. He lowered his head and kissed one, then the other, before opening his mouth to suckle her.

A blast of wet heat engulfed Amanda as she arched her back to give him better access as he feasted. His mouth claimed each side in turn, licking, nipping, blowing cool air across her fevered flesh. His hands reached into the opening of the teddy at the bottom and kneaded her buttocks, and then his fingers found her. She was slick with desire, ready for him. Amanda stiffened with pleasure from his gentle probing.

"Easy," he muttered against her breasts. "Slow and easy . . ."

Suddenly, Amanda was overcome with the need to touch him, too. She ran her hand over his chest, grazing his male nipples with her fingernails as she scratched her way down his body. The towel impeded her descent. She tugged at the intrusion and pushed it out of her way. Slowly she ran her fingertips over the length of him, and was rewarded with a satisfying groan. He was smooth and warm, and he filled her hand as she wrapped her fingers around him and caressed him.

Vince covered her hand with his own and stopped her movements. "If you keep this up, sweetheart, this is going to be over before it's begun."

Amanda smiled up at his self-mocking grin, joyous in her power over him. Obligingly she moved her hand away and ran it up and down the length of his body. She felt the puckered flesh on his right side before she saw it, and leaned forward. Vince pushed her away.

"Don't," he said.

Amanda recalled the commendation mentioned in his file.

"Is that where you were shot?"

"Yeah." He didn't seem surprised she knew. "The bullet went clear through. I came out of it okay, but it's not a pretty sight."

Amanda rose up onto her knees and pushed his hand away as she hovered over him. Gently she outlined the scar with her fingers, touching it with a feather-light caress. She replaced her fingers with her lips and kissed the area lovingly.

"Amanda, don't . . ."

He pulled her up to face him.

"I want to. I want to touch you all over." She cupped his face in her hands. "Don't you understand? I want to know, touch, feel everything about you."

They stared into each other's eyes for a long moment. She thought she saw a slight glistening in his eyes at her words, but before she could be sure, Vince's mouth captured hers in a devouring kiss, and all thoughts fled as his tongue touched and tangled with hers.

He rolled her over, tugged on the bottom of the teddy and flung it across the bed. She lay naked beneath him, and their bodies strained against each other, seeking completion. Amanda parted her legs to accommodate him and stared up into his mesmerizing slate eyes.

She touched his face with the palm of her hands. "Vince, I'm not using anything, no protection."

He bent his head and kissed her forehead before shifting his weight from her. He leaned over the side of the bed and pulled open the top drawer of the nightstand, taking out a small square package. Vince knelt between her legs and ripped open the foil just as Amanda reached up and gripped his wrist to stop him.

"May I?" she asked.

Vince felt the heat rush to his face as he handed the packet over to her. Silently, eyes never leaving his, Amanda slowly performed the intimate gesture for him. By the time she was finished, each feature on his face was taut with blatant desire. He fell forward onto her, and she arched her body to accept the powerful initial thrust as he entered her.

Fully joined, Vince looked into her eyes almost in disbelief that now, finally, she was his as he had dreamed of since that first meeting, that first day. He lifted her head so her mouth could find his, and they kissed deeply as their bodies began to move.

Amanda reveled in the feel of him inside her, filling her, spinning her out of control. It had been so long, but as she felt the passion building, she knew why there had been no other man since her divorce. She had been waiting for this feeling, for him. For Vince.

She climbed higher to the peak of fulfillment, and called out his name over and over again as spasms of joy rocked her body. As Vince absorbed the after-shocks of her pleasure, she hugged him tightly to her. When he joined her in completion, Amanda rubbed and massaged the tight muscles of his back and but-tocks as he whispered words of praise in her ear.

Vince allowed his full weight to rest on her for a moment as his pulse rate ran down to normal. He was almost afraid to look at her, afraid she might see the look of wonder on his face. For he was truly in awe of what they had just shared. She'd touched something in him, something deep, abiding and beyond the physi-cal. It scared the hell out of him.

Raising his head, he looked at Amanda's upturned face. Her eyes were closed. A small hint of a smile curved her lips. Her cheeks were flushed, and a light sheen of perspiration gave her skin a luminous glow.

Slowly, Amanda lifted her lids. Their gazes locked. Vince wanted to say just the right thing to her, but the words eluded him. What he felt for her at this moment was so new to him, so profound, that he could not ar-ticulate it. Instead he caressed the side of her face with the back of his hand. With a tenderness he hadn't known he was capable of, he placed a gentle, feather-light kiss across her lips.

"Amanda—"

"Shh..." she said as she hugged him tightly. "Don't say anything ... not a word."

He returned the hug, moving to alleviate her from the weight of his body, all the time keeping them joined together. Side-by-side, they stared into each other's eyes, content, happy...confused.

"Stay with me tonight," he said.

"I can't. The kids will be home in the morning."

"I'll set the alarm and get you up. I promise."

Amanda shook her head. "No, Vince, really. I have to go."

"Why?"

How did she tell him? Her emotions were in an uproar—tossing, turning, jumbling together as if in a blender. She couldn't spend the night with him, sleep with him, make love with him again. It was impossible...dangerous. She needed time alone, to think, to sort out what had happened, to relive the night step-by-step and come to terms with it.

She hesitated. "I just think it would be better if I left."

She hadn't answered his question, Vince realized, but he reluctantly accepted her need to go. He pulled her flush up against him and held her tightly. Their eyes met as he felt himself stir inside her; he knew she felt it, too. He also knew if she stayed a minute longer, they'd be making love all over again until dawn cast its dim light through the window of the cottage. Letting her go now was one of the hardest things he'd ever done. It shook him to the core to admit it to himself. He more than wanted her to stay: he wanted to absorb her whole.

They separated. Vince lay still under the light bedsheet and watched Amanda quickly don her clothing. He swung his legs over the side of the bed and reached for a pair of jeans lying across a chair.

"I'll follow you home," he said.

Amanda quickly zipped up her skirt and threw her coat over her arm. "No, Vince." She put out a hand to stop him. "It's okay. It's only a ten-minute drive. Please stay here."

"I don't like the idea of you driving alone in the dead of night like this."

As soon as the words left his mouth, he wondered where they came from. He had never been an overly cautious person. It seemed silly to be so concerned over a short drive through a sleepy town, but he was.

"I'll be fine," she said, and pulled the strap of her bag over her shoulder. She smiled awkwardly. "I don't know what to say. Is thank you appropriate?"

Vince dipped his head and kissed her lips. "I should be thanking you, I think." He kissed her again, more deeply this time.

A sweet thickness invaded her senses, and she forced herself to pull away. "I've got to go...."

Vince reluctantly released her, frustrated in his attempt to change her mind. He walked her out the door and stood on the rickety wooden front steps of the cabin. The predawn sky was beginning to lighten to a pale gray as she turned and headed toward her car.

"Go back inside," she said. "You'll get a chill."

God, she thought, you sound like his mother! She saw the amused grin on his face, and she knew he understood her discomfort with the situation. Amanda looked down at the bundle of keys in her hand and picked through them in pretended search of the correct one.

"Amanda..."

She looked up at his once again solemn expression. He was so handsome standing here so disheveled, so satisfied, and suddenly so beloved, a lump formed in her throat at the sight. She could only nod her reply.

"No regrets," he said softly, his voice drifting over her in the damp morning air.

She closed her eyes for a moment and bit her lower lip before opening the car door. Looking him straight in the eye, she shook her head.

"No regrets."

Eight

———

Hey, Mom, look!''

Amanda watched her son demonstrate a basic Tae Kwon Do move. She raised her eyebrows and grinned, nodding her approval of his accomplishment.

Her gaze strayed to the man standing behind Sean, and her smile slowly faded. Vince looked like a stranger in the stark black karate outfit, unknown and possibly dangerous. She studied him thoroughly, from his bare feet all the way up to the slate-gray eyes. He stood perfectly still and silent while she examined, as if he acknowledged her right to do so.

Their eyes met and held for a potent moment. Suddenly a brief flash darted across her mind, causing an involuntary shiver. The vivid picture of him poised above her made her face burn and her heartbeat accelerate. She wanted to walk over to him, reach out with her hand and touch his face, trace each feature with her finger. The impulse was so powerful and urgent, she curled her hands into fists to stop herself.

"Mr. Simpson..." Vince addressed Sean, his eyes never leaving Amanda's flushed face. "Line up."

Sean immediately ran back into a line of eight boys, aligning himself perfectly toe-straight. As Vince turned his attention back to the lesson, Amanda marveled at the sight. Sean never moved that quickly for her, no matter how forcefully she called. Perhaps it was an inherent response to a male voice, or perhaps it was just Vince's uniquely understated authority that prompted such obedience.

Amanda glanced at her watch. There were ten minutes left before the class was over. She leaned against the wall and watched as a stern and professional Vince reviewed the night's exercise.

He shouted, and all eight children shouted back at him in unison. Following his lead, the boys then punched out with their first two knuckles extended. Each boy brought his right foot to the rear, then kicked up and out, bare toes curled.

Amanda followed Vince's agile movements as he repeated the maneuver in slow motion for the boys' benefit. The loose-fitting karate suit hid his physique, but her overactive imagination filled in the details all too accurately.

It was amazing what one night of lovemaking could do, she mused, and smiled to herself.

"Reit," Vince said, concluding the lesson with a bow.

The boys bowed ceremoniously to him in return. He then clapped his hands together effectively ending the class for the night. "Good job! See you all next week, same time."

The children dispersed and greeted their parents who had filtered into the firehouse basement sporadically during the last few minutes. Sean ran over to Amanda, exhilaration beaming from his face.

"Did you see me, Mom? Did you? I was real good, wasn't I? I can't wait to get home and show Kim. She won't believe it!"

"Calm down." Amanda laughed and rubbed his hair. "You're going to jump out of your skin if you don't!"

"He's doing very well."

Amanda looked up at Vince as Sean ran off with his friend.

"I can see that. I'm very impressed."

Amanda smiled to cover her nervousness. Her stomach was in knots. She hadn't realized how awkward and ill at ease she'd feel seeing him again after Saturday night. Of course he'd called her the next day; he was too much of a gentlemen not to. But the kids and her brother were there, and she could only politely exchange small talk with him about Liddy's party. They hadn't really *talked* at all.

Part of her was glad; because while she knew things would now be different between them, she wasn't quite sure in what way. For, after all, what had really changed? She was still a single mother raising her kids in a small town. He was still a temporary sheriff on his way back to New York City.

She tried to be nonchalant and casual. They were adults, she told herself, consenting adults; and what had happened at the cabin had been her choice. They had been intimate—deeply, irrevocably intimate—but in the true scope of their lives, it didn't change a thing.

Then why was her heart beating triple time at just the look in his eye?

Vince reached out to take her hand as another parent called to him. "Sheriff? Can I talk to you for a minute?"

Vince turned. "I'll be right with you." He leaned toward Amanda. "Don't leave yet. I have to talk to you."

"I can't. Kim's waiting—"

"Five minutes." He held up his hand. "Please."

Nodding, she watched as he walked over to the other parent and shook hands. She called to Sean, who was now running wild around the basement. One by one the other parents and children left, until she stood alone with only Vince and the man he was talking to. She felt conspicuous and self-conscious. What did he want?

Don't be a fool, Amanda. You know what he wants. You know what you want....

"Thanks for waiting."

"It's okay," she said. "Did you want to talk about Sean?"

Vince tilted his head in disbelief and gave her an almost imperceptible shake. "No, Amanda. I don't want to talk about Sean. I want to talk about us—you and me."

"What about us?"

He laughed. "'What about us?'"

"That's what I said."

His laughter died, and his eyes became serious. "I want to see you again. Soon. Tonight."

"I can't to—"

"Then this weekend."

"Vince…please. Sean's birthday is Friday, and I'm having six boys for a sleep-over party. Believe me when

I tell you that I won't have any energy left on Saturday for anything." She stared into his eyes. "Least of all you."

"I'll take that as a compliment," he said with a grin. "Need any help with the party?"

Sean ran up and grabbed her arm. "Can we go now?" he interrupted.

"In a minute," she said to the boy, then returned her attention to Vince. "Thanks for the offer, but I'm sure you'd rather spend your evening relaxing instead of dealing with a bunch of ten-year-olds."

"Let me be the judge of that."

"Wow! Sheriff? Are you coming to my party? Maybe you could do a karate lesson. Wouldn't that be great, Mom? Cory'd be so jealous!"

"Sean, no. I'm sure the sheriff doesn't want—"

"I'd love to."

He stared at her intently, and she wondered what was going on in his mind. He had to realize that if he came to the party, they'd have no time alone. Her experience with men did not include those who enjoyed being with children for long periods of time. She supposed it was natural that she question his motives, but there was only one way to find out.

"If you're sure . . ."

"I'm sure. What time?"

"About six, six-thirty. We're getting pizzas and renting movies."

"I'll be there."

"Wow!" Sean said and jumped around the room.

Amanda looked Vince in the eye, trying to determine what he was up to. The feelings she saw shook her to the core as his gaze caressed her face.

She agreed with Sean. Wow.

* * *

"Pizza man!"

Amanda shook her head and opened her front door wide to allow Vince and five pizza boxes room to pass.

"What on earth...? How many did you get?"

He put the pizzas on the coffee table. "I bought extra for Kim and for us."

"Kim's staying over at a friend's house. She refused to be in the house with the animals. That's a direct quote," Amanda said.

"Well, don't worry about it going to waste. I'll bet there isn't a piece left over. By the end of the night they'll be nibbling on it cold." He glanced around the empty living room, then kissed her on the nose. "Hi."

He was a big man and certainly not the type you'd called "cute," but that was how she thought of him right now. Adorable. Boyish. Hers.

The door opened, and two of Sean's friends poked their heads in. Amanda forced her attention away from Vince to talk to the parents. Before she finished her first conversation, the remaining boys arrived and Sean bounded down the stairs to greet them as all hell broke loose.

Amanda sighed. No matter how hard she planned, or how well organized she was, it always seemed as if she lost control at the last minute.

Vince stood back and grinned at her attempts to calm the six rambunctious boys. She kept talking to them, directing them to sit and eat the pizza before it was cold, but they ignored her, talked over her and generally ran wild. He'd give it a minute, he thought, before stepping in. Right now he only wanted to look at her, drink his fill.

God, she was beautiful. Even in jeans and a sweat-shirt, she set his juices flowing. She bent to set the paper plates around the coffee table, and he admired her well-rounded derriere. She looked exasperated and ready to scream. It was time.

"Okay, you guys. Sit and eat the pizza." All eyes in the room turned to him. "Now."

Six little boys moved at once, vying for position around the coffee table. They sat cross-legged and patiently waited their turn as Amanda served them slices.

"How do you do that?" she asked as she walked over to him.

Vince shrugged. "It's my face, I think. They look at me and don't know exactly what I'll do if they don't comply. They decide it's not worth it to find out."

"It's not your face."

"No?" He leaned it toward hers until only an inch separated them.

"No. It's your eyes that scare them."

"Do they scare you?" he whispered.

Amanda returned his intent look. "Sometimes."

"Like now?"

"Are you *trying* to scare me?"

"Uh-uh. I'm trying to seduce you."

She laughed. "I don't think the atmosphere is conducive to seduction, Sheriff." She pointed to the six boys new devouring their second piece of pizza.

Vince sighed. "I guess not." He brought his hand up and rubbed his thumb across her lower lip. "Maybe later?"

She fought a raging desire to grab his hand and drag him upstairs to the bedroom.

"Mommmm. Can we watch a movie now?"

Amanda turned to see six pair of eyes staring at her and Vince.

"Uh, sure. Let's see what we have here." She walked toward the television and sorted through the three tapes Sean had picked out at the video store. Each title seemed worse than the next. "These are all horror movies!"

"Come on, Mom!" Sean pleaded.

"Let me see," Vince said as he walked up behind her. He chose a particularly gory-looking one and slipped the tape into the VCR.

"Vince! These boys are only ten years old."

He pressed the button to start the movie, and the boys cheered. Vince flipped off the light switch and took hold of Amanda's hand, dragging her protesting body toward the kitchen.

"Leave them alone, Amanda. Kids love horror movies. Don't you remember?"

"No," she said as she poured glasses of wine for Vince and herself. "I never watched them."

"Not even when you were a teenager at the drive-in? Didn't any date ever take you to a horror show so that you would crawl all over him at the scary scenes?"

"No."

He smiled devilishly and pulled her onto his lap. "Remind me one of these days to rent one and invite you over."

"Want me to crawl all over you at the scary scenes?" she teased as she put her arms around his neck.

"You can crawl all over me anytime. Anytime at all."

He kissed her. Amanda opened her mouth for him, and he took full advantage of the opportunity. Her body was soft, supple against him, and her lips were warm and compliant. Vince shifted in the kitchen chair to gain better access to her and deepened the kiss. He felt like a drowning man going down for the third time as he slipped further and further under her spell.

These last few days away from her had been torture for him. Denying himself, he'd come to realize, was not one of his strong points. But then, he'd never felt the need to have a woman, any woman, as strongly as he did Amanda.

He reached down to the small of her back and pressed himself into her. He was already aroused; every time he'd thought about her in the last three days, he'd become instantly aroused. And he thought about her all the time.

Amanda broke the kiss. "I'd better check on the boys," she said breathlessly.

"They're fine."

She pulled away from him and moved from his lap. "They may be. But I'm not."

He took her hand and kissed the palm. She pulled away and peeked into the living room. The six boys were staring intently at the screen as a man in a hockey mask terrorized a group of teenagers.

The front door opened, and she walked over to Polly, who stepped inside.

"Hi. I just stopped by to see if you needed any help," Polly whispered as she followed Amanda into the kitchen.

"Hi, Polly," Vince said as she entered the room.

Polly turned and shared a meaningful look with Amanda. "I can see you have all the help you need."

The three adults shared the wine and conversation until the movie was over. Sean came bounding into the kitchen to ask Vince to do the karate lesson with them and he complied, after they cleared away the furniture to make room.

Polly and Amanda stood on the sidelines watching Vince instruct the boys in the basic moves.

"Look at Sean's face," Polly said. "He looks at Vince as if he's a god."

"I know."

"You sound worried."

"Wouldn't you be? What will happen to Sean when he leaves?"

"I'm more concerned about what will happen to *you* when he leaves." Amanda found Polly's stare unnerving. "Something's changed, hasn't it, Amanda?"

Amanda nodded.

"When?"

"Saturday night. After Liddy's party." She looked her in the eye. "I went to his cabin."

"Are you in love with him?" she asked.

"I don't know if I'd call it love exactly," Amanda said, "but what I do feel is strong. Oh, Polly, it's getting stronger by the day. Every time I look at him . . ."

Polly put her arm around her. "Then don't fight it. Let it happen. It's about time, don't you think?"

"I'm scared," she whispered desperately.

Both women turned their attention back to Vince.

"Don't be," Polly said. "I don't really know much about him, but from what I can see, he's a good man. And good men are hard to find. Don't throw him away, Amanda. You may never find another like him."

It was after midnight before they had the boys bunked down on the living-room floor in sleeping bags. Polly had left hours ago, and Vince and she had cleaned up as best they could with the boys still in the house. Amanda walked Vince to the front door. He pulled her jacket off the hook and wrapped it around her.

"Come outside on the porch with me for a minute," he said.

The air was cool and dry and the moon full. Amanda slipped her arms into her jacket to ward off the chill as she peeked through the living-room window to check on the kids.

"They're not sleeping, you know," she said.

"They'll pretend for a while," he answered. "Don't you know half the fun of a sleep-over is not sleeping at all?"

"Easy for you to say. You can go home and go to bed. I have to keep one ear and one eye open all night."

"I'll stay if you want me to."

Oh, she wanted him to all right, but not with six ten-year-olds in the house.

"No. You were great with them tonight. Thank you for all your help. The boys had a ball."

"I enjoyed it, too. They're nice kids." He pulled her into his arms. "When will I see you again?" he asked.

"I—I don't know."

"Next weekend I'm planning to take some time off. Let's go somewhere together, Amanda. Alone."

"Vince," she protested, "I can't. I made plans—"

He nuzzled her neck and nipped her earlobe as he leaned her against the porch railing. "Change them."

His body was touching hers in all the right places. Amanda closed her eyes and savored the feel of him against her.

"Come away with me," he entreated, his breath stirring a curl at her temple.

"It's out of the question," she said with a calmness she didn't feel, as the mere thought of spending an entire night with him took her breath away. "I can't just go away with you. What'll I do with the kids? And besides, John is taking me to look at new cars next Saturday. The plans are all set.''

"Tell John I'll take you. I'll bet he and Polly will watch the kids if you ask. Come away with me, Amanda, please. Overnight. All night.''

"You're insane," she whispered halfheartedly as he brushed his lips against hers.

"Yeah, I am. Absolutely crazy. And it's all your fault." He rubbed his hands up and down her back. "Amanda...please. I want to hold you, sleep with you, make love with you again."

"Oh, God," she moaned. "I can't—"

"Say yes."

"I don't—"

"Just yes."

He kissed her again, and her body swayed into his as she reached around him and splayed her hands across his back. His tongue dipped into her mouth and claimed it thoroughly. The heat of his body radiated out, searing her to the core.

"Yes?" He broke the kiss, but kept his lips on hers.

"Yes . . ."

Hester Waterbury's front light flicked on, and Amanda broke away. "I have to go."

Vince moved toward the porch steps. "We'll go to the mountains. I'll call you as soon as I make the arrangements."

"Vince . . ."

He pressed his index finger onto her lips to silence her. "You said yes already. Don't say anything else. Good night, Amanda."

Nine

—

The hotel appeared before her like a castle out of a dream. The light, misty rain caused low level fog to obscure her vision as they rounded a particularly sharp curve. Tall pines lined the newly paved road, but Amanda was still able to catch glimpses of the impressive structure through the gaps in the branches.

She couldn't believe Vince picked this place to stay. It was an old, well-known hotel that had closed down years ago and fallen into disrepair. Her family had vacationed here many times when she and her brother were children. She had always felt like Cinderella running in and out of the nooks and crannies that combined to make up one of the most unique, if not baroque, hotels in the Catskills.

It was only recently that a group of wealthy investors had pooled their resources to renovate the resort and restore it to its previous glory. From what Amanda

could see from this distance, they'd more than succeeded. As the snakelike road finally straightened, she
caught her breath at the magnificent sight of the tur-
reted wonder.

"Oh, Vince . . . isn't it beautiful?"

"Bring back memories?" he asked.

She turned her attention to him. "How did you
know I'd been here before?"

"I asked John for suggestions on where to take
you."

"My *brother*? You asked my brother for a place
to . . . for us to . . ."

"Spit it out, Amanda."

"You know what I mean!"

Vince glanced her way and laughed. "Yeah, I did.
John was a great help."

Amanda made a face. "So that's why he and Polly
were so excited about the weekend! They agreed so
quickly about watching Kim and Sean, they almost fell
over each other to answer first."

"So, your brother approves of me. Anything wrong
with that?"

"My brother may be reading more into this than
either of us wants. He and his wife are die-hard
matchmakers and incurable romantics."

He stopped the car in front of the valet sign and
turned to her. His eyes were dark and turbulent, like
thunderheads before a storm. "You got anything
against romance?"

Amanda swallowed and mechanically shook her
head from right to left. "No."

"Good," he whispered. "Because in the next twenty-
four hours, you're going to O.D. on it."

"I am?"

"Uh-huh. Beginning now."

He opened his hand to her. Slowly she placed her own in his. Vince brought it up to his mouth and gently brushed his lips against her knuckles. When he was through, their gazes caught and held in promise and wonder. Amanda's pulse began to quicken. It was all she could do not to throw herself into his arms.

"Let's go," he said, and motioned to the valet to open the car door.

Hand-in-hand, they entered the huge lobby of the hotel. Amanda's heels tapped a staccato rhythm across the marble-tiled floor. Ornate gold leaf gargoyles glared at her from the corners of the cathedral ceiling. She stood back and absorbed the atmosphere as Vince signed the register. Pointing to the heavy furniture and velvet draperies with Florentine tassels, she tugged on his arm like a child at a country fair. Vince felt pleased with his choice and grinned at her enthusiasm as they followed the bellboy to the elevator.

Amanda perused the restaurant menu displayed in a glass-enclosed case on the wall. "Look, they have a special Sunday Brunch. Let's see," she said. "What'll you have tomorrow morning? The Eggs Benedict? Or—"

Vince pulled her into the elevator as it arrived. "Neither," he said.

"Can't make up your mind?" she teased.

"Uh-uh." He brought his lips to her ear. "I know *exactly* what I'm having for breakfast tomorrow. And it's not Eggs Benedict."

Amanda blushed and turned her face into Vince's sleeve. She felt as excited as a bride and couldn't wait to get to their room. Her clothes were chafing. She wanted to undress, lie on cool, freshly laundered sheets and make love all afternoon.

She fidgeted as the bellboy opened their door. She paced as he laid out their suitcases and checked the room. She feigned interest in the view of the garden from the window until she heard the click of the lock. Then she turned to face Vince.

"How do you like it?" Vince asked, his hand sweeping the room.

The room was large and airy. Two windows with billowing white voile curtains took up the outer wall. An antique highboy stood catty-corner near the arched entrance to the bathroom. The bed was double-size, with a white pleated dust ruffle covered by an embroidered white chenille bedspread. Two huge pillow shams rested against an intricately carved solid oak headboard.

Amanda walked toward the bed and sat down on the edge. She ran her hand over the nubby material and outlined a leaf with her finger. Vince came to stand in front of her, and she reached for his hand.

"It's so beautiful. So perfect. Like a dream."

He knelt down in front of her and wrapped his arms around her waist. Amanda held him to her, his head cradled against her breasts as she breathed in his scent. She closed her eyes and ran her fingers through his hair, then placed a soft kiss on the top of his head.

Vince's blood pumped hot and fast. He moved his hand around to her soft round belly and caressed her before moving up her side. He halted the motion just below her breast. As much as he wanted to make love with her, now was not the time. He had a plan, an entire sequence of events he wanted to share with her this day and night.

It was important to him to do this for her and for himself, too. For if truth be told, he had never been the type of man who indulged in romantic fantasies. Sex was very physical for him; and though he had been considerate of the women he'd been with in the past, he had never been inclined to involve himself in such frivolity as this.

But Amanda wasn't just anybody. She was special; too special, he told himself. Yet no matter how many times he sang himself the warning tune, the results were the same. She'd gotten under his skin, in his mind, in his heart, and he couldn't shake the feeling that he was going to be hard pressed to walk away from her when his time in Branchport came to an end. This weekend was as much for him as for her. He knew he was going back to New York, but he needed to take a part of her back with him, even if that part was only a memory.

And if that was the case, he was going to make sure it would be one hell of a memory for both of them.

"Come on," he said as he rose to his feet and pulled her up from the bed.

"Where are we going?"

"Outside."

"It's raining."

"Only a little. Don't worry, you won't melt," he said, grinning.

"Vince." Amanda followed him into the hallway. "I thought you and I . . . we were going to . . ."

He pulled her to him and pressed his body lengthwise into hers. "Patience." He nipped her earlobe. "Everything in good time, my lady."

She punched his chest playfully, and he laughed out loud at her forlorn expression. "Come on," he said as he hit the elevator button. "Show me around this place."

She did. She took him around the grounds through the English garden where tiny green buds were just beginning to peek out through the soil. Like children, they chased each other in and out of the maze of sculptured hedges where Amanda discovered a long-forgotten overgrown towpath that led to the lake. Single file, they followed the trail of trodden pine needles until a clearing appeared.

The fine mist had turned into a steady rain, and soon they were soaked to the skin. A cast-iron gazebo stood raised off the ground at the edge of the clearing, and Vince led her toward the enclosure.

"I'm freezing!" Amanda held out her arms and watched the water drip off her fingertips.

Vince opened his jacket and pulled her to him as he wrapped the leather around her.

"Better?" he asked.

She burrowed deeper into his chest, inhaling the fragrance of soap, leather and man. "Much."

The only sound was the pitter-patter of the rain on the metal roof. Vince rubbed his hands briskly up and down her back. "It's so quiet here, so peaceful. It seems like another world."

Amanda lifted her head to look at his face. "Too quiet for you?"

"A little," he said, "I don't think I could take a steady diet of it."

"A nice place to visit . . . ?"

Vince grinned. "Something like that."

"You miss the city." A sudden pang gripped her as she waited for his answer.

He nodded. "Yeah. I guess I do. There's always something going on, always people around." He shrugged. "I guess I'm just used to it."

"As I'm used to this," she said softly.

"Have you ever thought about moving away from Branchport again?"

"No. It took all that moving around with Billy to make me realize how much I love it here. I feel safe, secure." She broke away from his embrace and leaned against the gazebo's railing. "I don't worry about my children when they go to school, or out to play. It's the way I was brought up, and I want the same thing for them." She looked him straight in the eye. "I *am* happy here."

"Don't you feel you're missing out on a lot of life?"

Amanda laughed. "Not at all! From what I've seen, the parts I'm missing are not worth much in my opinion."

"Does that go for men, too?"

Amanda tilted her head and smiled. "Are you referring to yourself?"

"What if I am?"

"I'd say it's a little silly to talk about it since you won't be around much longer anyway."

"Does that still bother you?"

"I'd be lying if I said I don't think about it, but since...since we've made love...well, I've made my choice, Vince. I want you. Want to be with you. For however long that is. That's all that matters to me now." She was pleased with her answer. She sounded mature, self-confident, everything she should be.

"And when I leave?" He knew he was deliberately baiting her, but he needed to know.

Amanda took a deep breath and wrapped her arms around herself to ward off the chill. "I'll survive," she said with more bravado than she felt.

"Come here," he said, and she returned to the comfort his arms provided. "You're a very independent lady, Mrs. Simpson," he whispered into her hair.

"I've had to be, Sheriff,"

She offered her lips to him, refusing to ruin the day or the moment with thoughts of his leaving. Vince readily accepted the invitation to explore the depths within. He deepened the kiss, and she nestled her body in between his legs, seeking his warmth, feeling his desire. Breaking away, she kissed his chin, his neck, touching his Adam's apple with the tip of her tongue. Vince cupped the back of her head and pressed her to his chest as his head rested on top of hers. She could hear the steady pounding of his heart.

"I don't know about you," he said hoarsely, "but I think I've had about enough of nature for one day." Vince looked down into her bright brown eyes. "Let's go back to the room."

Eyes closed, Amanda relaxed as the hot water pelted her body, effectively erasing every last goose bump from her skin. She couldn't remember a day she'd enjoyed more. Even this morning during their trek through new and used car lots, she'd felt exuberant. She'd never thought that a mundane chore such as looking at cars could elicit such a response in her.

But it wasn't the cars, she knew; it was the man. He seemed to anticipate her every thought, her every wish. The only thing he hadn't been able to control was the weather, she thought with a smile, but despite the rain, all had been perfect.

Just being here at this place filled her with excitement. Ever since she'd been little, she'd imagined spending a romantic weekend at this resort, and here she was doing just that. A romantic weekend with a very special man . . . Vince. Thinking about him made her insides weak. Her body was heavy with longing for him, and she marveled at how quickly she'd become addicted to a man after all these years.

Maybe it *was* like riding a bike. . . .

A cool breeze hit her back. The shower curtain was pushed aside as Vince stepped into the tub.

"I'm sorry," he said.

"For what?" Her voice shook at the sight of his perfectly formed naked body.

"I couldn't wait. . . ."

He pulled her into his arms and kissed her. She reached up around his neck to hold him to her. The water cascaded over them as he deepened the kiss, his tongue exploring the recesses of her mouth, his lips teasing, his teeth nipping.

"Amanda . . . God . . . I ache for you."

Her insides turned to jelly with his words. As he rubbed a hair-roughened leg between her silky ones, her pulse rate took a dramatic leap. His hands glided over her slick body, massaging her breasts, rubbing her nipples, until little sharp stabs of pleasure assaulted her belly. Then his wet fingers found her, and she was completely lost. She kissed his chest, his shoulder, the curve of his arm in an almost-frantic attempt to devour him whole, all the while her body squirmed against his, seeking that ultimate fulfillment she craved.

Vince lifted her, and she wrapped her legs around his torso as he leaned back against the tiled wall. The heat of the water was nothing compared to the temperature between their two bodies, as with one quick thrust, he pushed into her.

For a tender moment they just stared into each other's eyes, slightly in awe of the tumultuous feelings they aroused in each other. But like two starved beggars at a feast, they couldn't stay still for long. As soon as he began to move within her, Amanda felt the spasms begin. She was so ripe, so ready, so hot for him, she couldn't control or temper her response.

He caught her moan in his mouth as his lips captured hers. Her movements were genuine and uninhibited, and he felt like a randy young buck instead of a grown man in control of his body.

"Amanda . . . sweetheart . . ."

And then he could say no more as he joined her in joyful completion.

Slowly she slid her weak legs down his sides. He supported her against his body for a timeless moment. Lost in an maelstrom of emotion neither would dare name, they held each other tightly, savoring the feeling.

Vince pushed the wet strands of hair from her face and stared at her. "I'm afraid I can't seem to keep my hands off you, Mrs. Simpson."

"I'm not complaining, Sheriff."

Amanda picked up the bar of soap and rubbed it into his chest hair. "Since you're already here . . ." she teased.

Mesmerized by the slow movement of her lathered hand against his chest, Vince managed a lazy grin. "Why do I get the feeling dinner is going to be late tonight?"

* * *

Dinner was late, and cold, but Amanda didn't mind at all. Vince suggested room service so as not to be too far away from the bed at any one given time in the evening. Amanda agreed wholeheartedly. They took turns tasting morsels of food, then each other. Sometime well after midnight the rain stopped and the luminous rays of the moon cast a pale glow across the antique bed as exhaustion finally claimed them.

Amanda felt his body jerk against hers before she heard the moan.

"Vince...?" she murmured, her mind drugged with sleep.

His body thrashed, and his arm shot out into the air. Amanda grabbed his shoulders and lay across him. "Vince! Vince. Wake up..."

Suddenly he sat up bolt straight, taking her with him. His eyes blinked several times before reality set in.

Vince looked down at the woman sprawled across his lap. "Oh..." he said, and ran a hand over his face. "I'm sorry. It was a bad dream."

Concerned, Amanda came up to her knees and wrapped the sheet around her torso. "Are you all right?"

"Yeah. Fine. Happens all the time. Don't worry about it. Go back to sleep."

She brushed some stray curls out of her eyes. "I don't think I can." Shutting her eyes tightly, she opened them again in an attempt to see his face in the darkness. "Do you want to talk about it?"

"No."

"I think you should," she said. "If not to me, then to someone."

He turned to her. "You think I need a shrink, too?"

"I didn't say that. Who thinks you need therapy?"

"My captain. He's the one who suggested this leave of absence. He says I should be over it by now."

"It?"

Vince swung his legs over the side of the bed and snapped on the light. He was visibly agitated. His hair was tousled; his face still showed evidence of sleep. He was unconcernedly naked as he walked over to the table and poured a glass of water. He offered it to Amanda with a gesture of his hand. She shook her head, and watched him as he took a sip. The sound of his swallowing was audible in the still room.

Vince studied her over the rim of the glass, trying to determine not only what to say, but how much. "Ed's death," he said. "My partner. I keep reliving that night."

"Why? Do you think you could have prevented it?"

He clunked the glass down on the table. "I don't know. Could I have?" He grabbed a pair of jeans hanging on the chair. He slipped them on, but didn't bother to fasten them as he paced in front of her. "I keep asking myself the same question. If I had acted differently, would they be alive today?"

"I thought Ed was the only one killed that night."

Vince stopped pacing. He stood before her, his thumbs hooked into his pockets. Could he—should he—tell her the truth? He had already gotten himself deeper into this conversation than he'd ever intended. But was she right? Did he need to talk about it? And if he did, was she the one with whom to open the floodgates? She'd made it perfectly clear to him that she abhorred violence of any kind. Should he take the chance of losing not only her respect, but the possibility that she could love him as much as he was beginning to suspect he already loved her?

Amanda's heart constricted as she recognized his inner turmoil. He needed her, and more than anything, she wanted to help him.

"Please, Vince. Trust me enough to tell me."

Vince stared at her for a long moment before falling to his knees in front of the bed. Amanda wrapped her arms around him and held him close to her.

"There was this kid," he said, his voice muffled as she cradled his head against her breast. "I found out later he was only fifteen. But I didn't know it that night. It was dark, cloudy, no moon. It had rained earlier. I remember that the streets were wet and shiny and the streetlights created a glare on the asphalt.

"Ed and I were checking out a robbery report. It was late, around two in the morning, and the business area was deserted. It happened so fast, I still can't get it all straight even in my own mind. We checked a broken lock on one of the buildings' lobby doors, and before I knew what was happening, two shots rang out.

"I didn't think. Hell! I didn't even look. I just reacted. I dove, spun around and fired. When it was over, Ed was hurt so bad he didn't make it to the hospital. And the kid . . . he died right there on the sidewalk. His mother had to come to identify the body. She wanted to see me, but I refused. I couldn't do it, couldn't look at her face . . ."

Amanda heard the hurt in his voice and the guilt. He had directed all the blame at himself because he had been the one to survive. He was wrong to feel so responsible, she knew; but she also knew that he didn't need to hear the same old platitudes that everyone else had been feeding him over the past two years. His feelings were strong, and they were real. To his mind, it was irrevocably his fault. Nothing she could say would change that.

Their eyes met. "It's not a pretty story," he said.

"No."

"I only wish I could go back to that night, that split second, and live it over again."

"But you can't," she said.

Vince's look was penetrating. "You're right. I can't."

She wanted to help him, and felt that by getting him to talk was a first, important step. But she also knew this was something only he could work out. He had to forgive himself.

"It won't go away, Vince. It's something you have to learn to live with. The memory will lessen in time, but for me to tell you it will disappear completely would be a lie."

"I know that. And it is getting better. The dreams *have* been coming fewer and farther between. Especially since coming to Branchport." *Especially since you.*

"You're a fine, good person," she said as she caressed his brow with her fingertips. "And in spite of the violence you've seen, you still have a gentleness. I see it in the way you are with the kids. The way you are with me. Don't let this eat you alive. You have so much to give." *And I want it all,* she added to herself.

Vince studied her face for a moment. There was none of the disgust he'd anticipated. His heart swelled with gratitude for her understanding. His emotions were raw, and he needed the healing balm only she could supply. He brushed his mouth across hers then moved down her neck to her collarbone.

He felt as close to her right now as he ever had to any other human being in his life. Her natural compassion for what he'd been through touched parts of him long dormant, or perhaps never even acknowledged. She'd thrown his well-ordered life completely off kilter. He wanted to tell her how much her listening meant to him, but since the words would not come easily to him, he showed her instead.

Amanda writhed beneath the scorching assault of his mouth as he left a trail of hot, wet kisses down her body. She arched her back when his fingers found and caressed her. In the midst of it all, she knew what he was doing, realized this was his way of thanking her for being there for him. As aroused as she was, she needed to let him know it wasn't necessary.

She knew how he felt; she felt it, too.

"Vince... You don't have to—"

He lifted his head and stared at her flushed face, all the while his fingers continued to work their magic. "Yes, I do," he whispered. "For me."

As his mouth and tongue replaced his fingers, all thoughts fled her mind. The sensations were so intense, she called out his name in surprise as jolts of pure pleasure racked her body. As he lifted her hips to feast on her, his name died in her throat, replaced by tiny whimpers of delight. Then a light burst across her mind, and a powerful spasm rocked her over the edge into a blinding climax.

Vince rose above her trembling body and held her to him. When he kissed her mouth, she tasted her essence combined with his own special flavor of man.

Unbidden tears rose to her eyes at the depth of her feeling for him.

It was no use. She was in love with him, and though she could never tell him, neither could she deny it to herself.

Ten

___

One look at her desk Monday morning shattered Amanda's hopes of it being an easy day. Greeting her were two stacks of reports decorated with myriad colored self-stick notes from Mike. Just her luck that he'd picked this weekend to catch up on his paperwork! She plopped her pocketbook down on the corner of the desk, slipped out of her jacket and rolled up her sleeves.

She poured a much-needed cup of coffee and began to sort through the work. After reading each sentence three times, she gave up the pretense of concentration. Thoughts of the weekend kept floating in and out of her mind, creating a warm inner glow that did more than distract her. Amanda replayed each touch, each kiss over and over again. She wanted more, much more than his time in town would ever allow.

With the light of day, reality had set in. There could be no more romantic weekends away. She couldn't afford to dream of Vince in her future. It served no purpose other than to depress her. All last night she'd tossed and turned in bed, battling the feeling of imminent loss, a loss that, surprisingly, was affecting her much more deeply than Bill's departure ever had. She couldn't give in to these feelings. She'd known the score from the beginning; he'd never made any false promises.

As she'd listened to him talk about the death of his partner and the boy, she'd recognized his need to return to the city. He had to come face-to-face with the ghosts that haunted him before he could ever go on with his life.

There was no time for second thoughts anymore. She'd made her choice. Yet each time she told herself it didn't matter, she'd get over him, his face would appear in her mind's eye, and the intense longing would return.

And he hadn't even left yet. What would she do when he did?

The phone rang.

"Mayor's office."

"Amanda? It's Hester Waterbury. I just called to tell you that I won't be going out tomorrow and I will be able to watch Sean for you."

"Well, thank you. That's a load off my mind!" Sean's school had a half day for teachers' meetings, and Amanda always hated leaving him at home alone. Hester had come through for her on more than one occasion.

"And you don't have to rush home from work. I'll make a special dinner for him, and Kimberly, too, when she comes home."

"Oh, Hester, you're doing enough already. You don't have to go to all the trouble of fixing dinner, too."

"No trouble at all. I want to. Don't get the chance to cook for more than one anymore."

"Thanks again."

"You're welcome."

After an awkward silence, it was apparent that Hester wasn't hanging up.

"Uh, was there anything else?" Amanda asked.

"I just thought you might want to talk for a minute. You know, about your weekend and all." Her birdlike voice rose to an excited shrill.

"My weekend was fine. How about you?" Amanda answered cautiously.

Hester giggled like a schoolgirl. "Oh, come now, Amanda. You can tell me."

"Tell you what?" As she asked the question, her throat constricted and she had to swallow hard.

"You know," the woman whispered. "About you and the sheriff. I'll bet we'll be hearing wedding bells sometime soon!"

Amanda shut her eyes and winced.

"Liddy told me all about it," Hester continued. "And I couldn't be happier. It's about time, Amanda. And he seems to be a fine young man."

"Hester, listen to me. The sheriff and I are just friends."

"Friends? Why that can't be. Liddy said—"

"I don't care what Liddy said, the truth is that we dated a few times and that's all there is to it."

"But I thought . . . oh, dear. Then I suppose that means there won't be any wedding?"

"Right. No wedding."

"Everyone will be so disappointed!"

"Everyone?"

"Well, I certainly didn't call *everyone*, but, oh dear. I'd better hang up. I'll see you tomorrow, Amanda."

Amanda heard the click in her ear. She sighed as she cradled the receiver. It didn't take a genius to figure out that Hester had some phone calls to make. By nightfall the town would be buzzing once again about the state of Amanda's love life.

She really was going to have to scratch Liddy's eyes out one of these days. There was only one way she could have found out, and that was through Sam. And how did Sam know?

Grabbing her jacket, she stormed out of her office and out the door to the other side of the municipal center complex. Without acknowledging any of the other officers in the police station, she made a beeline for the beveled glass door marked Sheriff.

The door flew open, and Vince looked up at the woman before him. "Amanda—"

"How could you?"

"What—"

"How could you? After all I've told you. After all you know about this town and the people around here. I don't belive I could do this to me!"

"Do what? Amanda, stop pacing, for pete's sake, and sit down."

"I can't sit down. I'm too mad to sit down! Lord! Don't you have a brain in your head? I have two children!"

"Amanda." He rose and came around the desk. Taking hold of her shoulders, he settled her in the leather chair in front of his desk. "Now, take a deep breath. Tell me what I've done." He leaned against the desk.

Amanda gazed at him with all the pent-up longing, confusion, and fury in her eyes. "You told Sam Halverson that we were away together this weekend, didn't you?"

"Of course I did."

"Of course you did! For heaven's sake, why?"

"He's my deputy. He has to know where I am at all times."

Amanda brought a fist up to her forehead and closed her eyes. "I don't believe this."

"I don't understand what the problem is."

Her eyes snapped open, and she leveled her best glare at him. "The problem, Sheriff, is that he tells Liddy everything. And now that Liddy knows, so will this entire town within twenty-four hours, if they don't already."

"I still don't see what's wrong. You're not a child, Amanda. Surely you're allowed to have a personal life."

"A personal life is one thing. Going away with a man for a weekend is something else entirely."

"This is ridiculous," he said and walked back around his desk in a dismissing action.

Amanda stood. "It is not ridiculous! Just wait and see." She ran a hand through her hair. "I'll have to get hold of Kim and warn her. And Sean! Who knows what the kids at school will say to him." She seemed to be talking to herself.

"Amanda—"

"No. Not another word. It's apparent you don't believe me." She turned to go, but stopped dead with her hand on the doorknob as a new thought came to her and warmed her to the core. Dealing with the town gossips was nothing new for her, but Vince? She turned, smiled serenely at him and nodded slowly. "But you will."

Vince watched as Amanda quietly shut the door behind her. "What the . . . ?"

Within minutes Sam poked his head in. "Problem, Sheriff?"

"No, Sam." Vince stood and picked up his hat. "I think I'll make some rounds. I'll call in, but don't expect me back until late."

"Okay," Sam said, then hesitated. "Sheriff?"

"What is it?"

"You still planning on leaving when Odus comes back?"

Vince's brows furrowed. "Sure. Why do you ask?"

"Well, we've been talking—" Sam motioned in the direction of the other deputies "—and we thought you might've changed your mind."

"Why would I do that?"

"You know . . . you and Amanda Simpson, and all . . ."

Vince couldn't believe his ears. His face hardened. "No, Sam, I haven't changed my mind. And even if I did, with Odus coming back, I'd have to take your job, now wouldn't I?"

Not waiting for Sam's reply, Vince left the station, but not before noticing the speculative glances thrown his way by the other deputies on duty. This was absolutely amazing! No one ever delved into his personal life on the job unless he volunteered information.

People just didn't *ask* those kinds of questions where he came from. He shook his head and laughed as he tugged the cap on.

"Branchport," he muttered out loud. "More like Peyton Place."

By the time the end of the week rolled around, Vince was convinced truer words had never been spoken. Every day during rounds, he'd listened to more than his share of remarks and innuendo regarding his relationship with Amanda. One elderly lady at the bank had caused him to blush to his roots when she came right out and asked him, "Why won't you marry her?"

He had to admit to himself that he'd always felt Amanda overreacted to the way people in town talked, but after the grueling two hours he'd just spent having lunch with Odus Tucker, he had to revise his earlier assumption.

That "little talk" during lunch today had been the topping on the cake. Father-to-son, Odus had stated unequivocally, you don't dally with the local ladies. *Dally!* For pete's sake, what the hell was *dallying*, anyway? Is that what he was doing with Amanda? He'd actually felt the sweat break out on his forehead while the man lectured. Never in his life had he had to sit through a talking-to like this one. He'd felt as if he should be looking over his shoulder for the shotgun to appear.

At first he'd laughed it off. It was comical to listen to each person's different bit of advice on his love life. But by the end of the week, he was more than annoyed. He was mad. What right did they have to judge either him or Amanda? How did she stand it? He shook his head. He'd do well to get himself back home and soon. But the thought of leaving Amanda left him cold. As useless as it was, he couldn't help but want to take her with him. Yet no matter how hard he tried, he couldn't picture Amanda or her kids living in his apartment in the Bronx.

He strolled into the municipal complex to see her. Dropping in on her unexpectedly seemed to be a habit he couldn't break. It was as if he needed his "Amanda fix" each day.

The door to the mayor's office swung open, and Vince stepped inside. Amanda's desk was empty and appeared cleared off for the night. Vince checked his watch; she'd probably left for the day already. Disappointed, he was just about to leave when Mike Powell came out of his office.

"Vince. How are you?"

"Fine, Mike. You?"

Mike nodded. "Fine, fine. Something I can help you with?"

"No, I was just leaving." Vince turned.

"Looking for Amanda?"

"What if I am?"

"Don't be so defensive, Vince. I'm not going to read you the riot act."

"Then you're the only one in town who isn't."

Mike laughed. "Folks been giving you a hard time, eh?"

"You could say that. Odus told me not to 'dally' with the local women."

"That sure does sound like Odus, all right. I know how you must feel, everyone breathing down your neck and all. But Branchport people feel special about their own. They want what's best for them. They also want to protect them." Mike walked up to Vince and looked him in the eye. "They'd hate to see Amanda hurt again. Me, too."

Vince acknowledged the mayor's challenge. "I've no intention of hurting Amanda."

"Glad to hear that," Mike said. "But you are still planning to leave when Odus returns, aren't you?"

"That's the deal. Amanda knew that from the beginning. I never lied about staying in Branchport. She's a big girl, Mike. She'll be fine," he said with more conviction than he felt about the state either one of them would be in when he finally packed his bags and returned to the Bronx.

"Maybe," Mike admitted, but his tone of voice belied the statement. "Have you told her?"

"You mean about Odus?"

"Yes. I spoke to him this afternoon."

"No. Not yet. And, Mike, I'd appreciate it if you let me tell her first."

The mayor nodded slowly. "Suit yourself. You know, Vince, you don't have to rush off next week when Odus comes back. He's a stubborn old bull and won't admit that he's not up to this job anymore. We could find a place for you here."

Vince shook his head and opened the door to leave. "Thanks, but no thanks, Mike. I think it's time I got back to the city. Something tells me I may have already overstayed my welcome in Branchport."

Amanda's head was pounding. Some people worked better under pressure, but she wasn't one of them. As this nightmare of a week had progressed, she'd sunk deeper and deeper into depression. She'd forgotten how trying it was to deal with gossips, and how much it took out of you to put on a happy I-don't-care face when all you wanted to do was run and hide.

She parked the car in her driveway and headed for the house. Her peripheral vision caught Hester Waterbury peeking through her blinds, but she chose to ignore her. Amanda slammed her front door behind her and leaned against it.

"Hi, Mom." Sean came up and hugged her.

Amanda returned the hug and kissed the top of his head. "Hi, buster. How was school?" She pulled back and looked at him. "Any problems?" It was the same question she asked every night.

"Nah," he said and walked back into the living room to his video game. "We had a math test. I passed."

"Great," she said, adding a prayer of thanks to her previous one that at Sean's age at least, kids didn't seem that interested in gossip. Anyway, if someone had said something to Sean, he was keeping it to himself and didn't look at all bothered by it. She thought it best to let sleeping dogs lie and not ask him directly.

She found Kim in the kitchen setting the table. She had already started dinner, and Amanda was grateful. Her daughter looked up as she entered the room and smiled.

"I thought you might need some help, Mom."

Amanda smiled. "How bad was it today? Same as yesterday?"

Kimberly shrugged. "No. Not too bad. Peggy and Marcia made some comments, but the other girls shut them up." She grinned at her mother. "You're kind of a celebrity, you know."

"A celebrity?"

"Yeah. All the girls in school have been falling all over themselves to get the sheriff to notice them ever since he came. They think he's real cute, you know? And you got him. It kind of makes you, I don't know... special. You know what I mean?"

"I think I do. But how do you feel about your mother being... special?"

Kim grinned. "I guess I never thought about you like that. I don't know. I think it's pretty neat."

Amanda hugged Kim, and together they finished making dinner. After they'd eaten, the phone rang, and Amanda sat back on the sofa to listen to her mother's long-distance lecture. She'd known this was coming all day. She'd met an old friend of her mother's at the luncheonette, and after they had exchanged small talk, the woman mentioned that she'd called her mother the night before. It was inevitable that the news would reach her ears.

After a lot of "Yes, Moms" and "No, Moms," she closed her eyes and relaxed against the couch as her mother rambled on with the familiar tune of how her reputation was now in tatters, and who did this man think he was to waltz into town and drag her good name through the mud?

Kim came downstairs and headed for the door midway through her mother's tirade. As her daughter waved goodbye, Amanda looked up and caught a glimpse of something on her jacket. Something like a piece of jewelry.

"Mom?" Amanda interrupted. "Let me call you back." She quickly cradled the receiver and met Kim at the door. "Where are you off to?" she asked as she eyed the lapel of her blazer.

"Over to Chris's to do homework. I told you, didn't I?"

"Oh, yes. You did. What's this?" Amanda toyed with the pin.

"Isn't it beautiful?" Kim asked. "Tommy gave it to me."

Amanda recognized the brooch immediately. It looked just like the one the Prine sisters had reported stolen. Its distinctive ivory cameo in a gold setting looked antique and expensive. Too expensive for Tommy Bronson to be giving away.

"Where did he get it?" Amanda asked softly, trying to control her anxiety.

"I don't know. He didn't tell me. He just said he wanted me to have it. I love it. I'm going to wear it every day."

"What you're going to do is take it off right now and come inside."

"What? Mom…" Kim said as Amanda dragged her toward the sofa. "What is it? I'm late already."

"And you're going to be later still." Amanda stood over her daughter. "Kimberly, this brooch is stolen. It belongs to the Prine sisters."

"That can't be, Mom. Tommy wouldn't steal anything."

"What about the shoplifting, Kim? You know it wasn't the first time he was picked up for that."

Kim sighed. "I know, but he didn't mean to when I was with him. He just forgot." Amanda raised her eyebrows, and Kim retaliated to the questioning gesture. "Well, he *did*!"

"I'm going to call Vince."

"No! Please, Mom, don't! If Tommy gets in trouble one more time, his parents are going to send him away."

"I have to. I can't handle this, and neither can you."

Ignoring her daughter's protests, Amanda dialed the phone.

"Hello?"

"Vince? It's Amanda. Can you come over?"

"Why don't you come here? I miss you—"

"Uh, no. I don't think so. This is business."

"What kind of business?"

"I think I have the Prine sisters' brooch."

There was a short, silent pause. "I'll be right over."

Kim stood and walked over to Amanda. "Maybe I should call Tommy?"

"No. Let's wait and see what Vince has to say."

"Do you think he'll arrest Tommy?"

Amanda put her arm around Kim. "I don't know, honey. Maybe."

"This isn't fair!" she shouted. "Tommy can't be the thief! I know it."

"Come on in the kitchen," Amanda said. "I'll make some coffee."

The doorbell rang just as the coffeepot began to perk. Amanda eyed Kim and headed out of the kitchen to answer it. She found Sean greeting Vince. He ruffled the boy's hair and caught her eye. So many unsaid words, she thought as she looked at his chiseled face, so many feelings.

"I've made coffee," she said and led him toward the kitchen. "Sean? Finish your homework, please."

The boy made a face, but complied, piling his books in a stack and heading up to his room.

Vince and Amanda entered the kitchen together as Kim nervously acknowledged his greeting.

"Let me see it." He held out his hand to Kim and she dropped the brooch into his palm.

Vince examined the piece of jewelry and nodded. "It sure looks like it."

"It has to be, Vince. It's too much of a coincidence not to."

"The question is, where would Tommy Bronson get hold of it?"

"He didn't steal it," Kim said with conviction.

"You seem sure of that," he said.

"I am." Kim looked him right in the eye defiantly, and he saw more than a little of her mother's determination in that look.

He nodded slowly. "I'm going to take this with me and go have a talk with the boy and his parents."

"Don't do that!" Kim raised her voice hysterically. "His parents threatened to send him away if he gets in trouble one more time. Please, Sheriff."

Vince stood, declining the offered mug of coffee in Amanda's hand with a shake of his head. "Kim, he's a minor. I have to tell his parents. I don't have any choice. But I promise you I'll listen to what he has to say. I'll give him the benefit of the doubt. Trust me. Okay?"

Kim eyed him for a moment. "Okay. You were fair the last time. I'll trust you. I guess you know what you're doing."

"Thanks for the vote of confidence." Vince smiled and put out his hand to the girl. "Friends?"

Kimberly managed a slight grin and nodded slightly as she put her hand in his and shook. "Friends."

Amanda touched his arm as Kim left the room. "Thanks," she said. "You handled that very well."

"Kim's a very loyal friend. I like having her on my side."

Amanda glanced at the brooch in his hand. "Call me after you've spoken to the Bronsons."

"Okay." He followed her to the door.

It was not the way he wanted to be with her tonight. He had so much to say, but now was not the time. He had to tell her he was leaving. Later, he thought, they'd talk later, after he straightened this out.

It turned out to be much later than either of them thought. Amanda had dozed for a while on the couch waiting for his call. Sean had become overtired and had a hard time falling asleep, so she'd let him come downstairs. Now he was fast asleep alongside her. He was too big to carry, and she was loathe to wake him. She'd ask Vince to bring him upstairs when he returned.

She sensed rather than heard the soft knock on the door. Uncurling herself from the couch so as not to wake Sean, she walked over and opened it a crack.

"Hi," he whispered.

The door swung open to admit him into the room.

"Hi."

He followed her past the sleeping boy into the kitchen, and this time accepted the mug of coffee. Sitting across the table from each other, they stared at the brooch Vince had placed on its center.

"Well? What happened?" she asked finally.

"It looks as if we've found the thieves."

"Tommy?"

Vince shook his head, took a deep breath and gave a mirthless laugh. "No. But he knows who they are and maybe even where they're staying. I brought him and his parents down to the station, and he pointed out a wooded area on the map about twenty miles south of town. Says two guys he met at the mall invited him to a house out there for a party about a month or so ago. They fed him a couple of beers and asked him a lot of questions." Vince shook his head. "Stupid kid. He didn't even realize they were pumping him. He's got such a hunger to fit in, he jumped at the chance to brag about all he knew about Branchport.

"We've known for a while that there were two of them. One of the guys is an ex-con out of Attica and the other one is his cousin. What we didn't know was where they were holed up. With all the summer houses up by the lakes, there were too many places for them to hide, and too much area for us to cover." Vince stood and poured the remainder of the coffee down the drain. "Both of them are in their early twenties. Tommy must have felt like a big man with them. They threw him the brooch and some cash. He says he didn't even know it was stolen."

"Do you believe him?" Amanda asked.

"After meeting his parents, yeah. They treat him like dirt. You know them?"

Amanda shook her head. "Not really. I met Mrs. Bronson at a P.T.A. meeting some years ago, but we never really talked."

"Well," he said, "it just goes to prove, you don't have to be an inner-city kid to be neglected. That boy is starving for attention and affection."

"Are you going to arrest him?"

"No, but I didn't tell his parents that. I told them they had to attend family counseling, or I'd charge him as an accomplice."

"Can you do that?"

"Hell, no! Only the D.A. can do that. But I put on my best cop voice and scared the pants off all of them. I think it'll work out if they'll just give it a try."

She believed him. Amanda grinned as she remembered how he'd handled the kids in the movie theater.

"Feel like taking a ride with me?" he asked.

"Where to?"

Vince picked up the brooch. "Sam called the Prine sisters and told them we have the brooch. They probably won't let me in the door dressed like this." He glanced down at his jeans. "Come along and help me out."

"Okay," she said. "Just let me tell Kim I'm leaving."

They tiptoed past Sean's sleeping form. "Leave him," Vince said. "I'll carry him up when we get back." At the front door, he turned and took her into his arms. "We've got some talking to do, you and me."

"I know."

"After we drop this off, if you're not too tired..."

Amanda nodded and planted a quick kiss on his lips.

Within minutes they were at the Prine's front door. Amanda knocked and waved as Lorna peered out the window. With agile speed of a woman half her age, Lorna welcomed them inside.

"Come in, come in. Amanda. Sheriff. Majorie and I are so excited! Aren't we, Majorie?"

"Oh, yes," said the timid, frail woman behind her. "We're very excited!"

Vince held out his hand. "Here it is, ladies."

Majorie gingerly picked up the brooch off his palm and cradled it between her two tiny hands. "Oh, Lorna, look. Nothing's happened to it. It's just as perfect and just as beautiful as ever."

Majorie looked up at Vince with tears in her eyes, too full of emotion to talk anymore. She nodded her thanks to him.

"How can we thank you?" Lorna asked.

"No thanks necessary, ma'am. It's my job."

"A job you do very well, Sheriff. I think this town is going to miss you very much."

Amanda smiled and patted Lorna's arm. "He'll be here a while longer, Mrs. Macahan."

"Oh, really?" she said. "I'd heard Odus was coming back on Monday."

Amanda's face fell, and she turned to stare in disbelief at a stone-faced Vince.

"Isn't that true, Sheriff?" The old woman continued.

Vince felt as if a stone had wedged itself in his throat. He had wanted to tell her himself, in his own way, in his own time. But why the hell should he be surprised? This town was always a step ahead of him in news of the day. He swallowed hard and nodded, his eyes never leaving Amanda's.

"Yes, ma'am, it's true," he said softly. "I'll be leaving next weekend."

Amanda didn't talk to him all the way back to the house. She'd cut him off each and every time he'd opened his mouth to speak. She was upset, angry, devastated, so much so that she didn't trust her voice to make any coherent sound.

Vince followed her into her kitchen and studied her stiff shoulders and straight back as she busily and meticulously lathered each of the mugs in the sink.

"When were you planning to tell me?" she asked, her voice soft and controlled.

"Tonight. When we were alone. When we had time to talk."

She shrugged, her back still to him. "There's really nothing else to say, is there?"

"We both knew this was coming, Amanda," he said, his voice ragged. "Odus has a right to come back if he feels able."

"I know." She dragged in a breath of air. "But I wasn't expecting it to happen this soon." She fought the tears that threatened.

Vince came up behind her and put both hands on her shoulders. He pulled her back to rest against him as his lips brushed her hair.

"Come back with me."

Her body stiffened. "You can't be serious."

"I am. I want you with me."

Amanda broke free and turned to him. "You don't know what you're asking. If it were only me I had to be concerned with, I'd be upstairs packing my bags now. You know that, don't you? But I have to think about the kids. Vince, they're finally settled, happy. I can't do this to them again."

"You mean you won't."

She stared at him. Her chin jutted out unconsciously. "Yes. I won't."

Vince ran a hand through his hair. "What is it you want from me, Amanda? Do you want me to leave the city and live up here?"

"I haven't asked you to stay, have I? I know you must go back. I know you have things to straighten out. And then..."

"Then, what? With Odus coming back, even if I wanted to, I wouldn't have a job here. What would I do?"

"I know. It's impossible. You don't belong here," she said.

"And you do."

She returned his penetrating look with one of her own. "Yes, I do."

The kitchen door swung open, and a sleepy Sean stood on the threshold, rubbing his eyes.

"Mom?"

Both Vince and Amanda turned to him.

"It's all right, sweetheart," she said. "Come on, I'll take you upstairs."

Vince came up behind her. "I'll carry him."

"No, please," she said, her face determined. "I'll do it myself."

Vince walked behind her as she led the boy to the stairway.

"Go on up, Sean. I'll be right there to tuck you in. The sheriff is leaving."

"Okay," Sean said. "See you next week, Sheriff."

"No, you won't," Amanda cut in. "The sheriff is leaving Branchport next week."

Amanda noticed his clenched jaw and knew he was annoyed at her hostile attitude. She couldn't help it. If she didn't keep her anger, she would cry, and she swore to herself that she wouldn't do that in front of him. Time enough for tears later.

"Don't worry, Sean," Vince said. "Someone else will be coming in to finish the session. You won't miss any classes."

"Leaving?" Sean said. "How could you be leaving Branchport, Sheriff?"

"Odus Tucker is coming back next week."

"Yeah. So?"

"Well, I have his job. When he comes back, I have to leave."

"But you can't! If you leave, how can you do what everyone told me you're going to do?"

"What's everyone told you, Sean?" Vince asked.

"That you're going to marry my mother."

Eleven

He'd known he was going to miss her; that was a given. He hadn't expected to miss the damn town, too.

Vince put his hands over his ears. They were arguing again. For at least the third time this week, the couple next door were involved in a screaming match that was driving him crazy. Had they always fought like this? He'd lived in this apartment for five years, but he didn't even know their names. They must have had many battles such as this, but he probably never noticed it before... before the quiet of Branchport.

A fire engine and police siren wailed through the streets. Vince checked his watch. One in the morning. The city never sleeps, and it looked as if neither would he tonight.

It had been more than a month since his return to the Bronx. One month, six days, five and a half hours to be exact, but who was counting? After the initial flurry of excitement that went with being back in town, life had predictably returned to normal. But what was normal before seemed confining and stifling now. And the future? The future appeared on the horizon as one huge gaping void.

Vince got up out of bed, a bed that all of a sudden seemed strange and uncomfortable. Someone was walking the floor in the apartment above him, and the footsteps startled him. Silly things such as that were happening all the time. Could three months away in that godforsaken town have changed him so? Had it made him this restless, this discontent? Or was it something else?

He'd heard people say you could be lonely in a roomful of people. Vince had never believed them. To him, those people didn't join in, didn't try to belong and made themselves miserable in return. But lately his mind was changing. Each time he went out to a club or to visit a group of friends, a wave of loneliness would engulf him sometime during the night. A yearning for something more meaningful than the shallow, trite personalities he'd always known and loved; deeper than the urbane banter that passed for intellectual conversation, but in fact was nothing more than self-aggrandizement. He'd become used to simpler ways of passing the time, simpler pleasures.

Maybe it was because he was more at peace with himself. The frantic urgency of city life didn't give him the high it had before. After catching up with family and friends, he'd been at loose ends, with too much time on his hands. He'd stopped at the station to check in. The captain deemed him ready to return, but he'd said no, not yet. Something inside was still unsettled, holding him back.

After the second week of self-imposed isolation, he'd admitted to himself what it was. He had to go see her—the mother of the boy he killed.

He'd found the address easily enough; he knew the neighborhood well. The apartment had been on the third floor of a restored tenement walk-up. It had been the most difficult climb he'd ever made in his life. He'd become out of breath, and his palms had sweated so much he'd had to wipe his hands on his shirt before knocking. When she'd opened the door, he'd been frozen to the spot.

She had recognized him immediately and had invited him in, a small sad smile on her face, as if she'd been expecting him all this time. She'd made him coffee, and they'd talked, long past the ten minutes he'd allotted himself to stay. He'd told her about his life, and she'd talked about her son—the little boy he was before the trouble started. In the process, he'd received the absolution his soul craved, and in turn, had given her the chance to understand what really happened that fateful night. By the time the sun began to dip behind the buildings, they'd formed a strange, irrevocable bond.

Even now he was still in awe of her generosity of spirit, of her ability to forgive and go on with her life. He felt as if a weight had been lifted off his chest; and although he knew he'd never forget the events of that night, he could finally come to terms with it. He accepted the fact that he was human and had reacted in the only way he knew how. It was over, and it was time to put the past behind him.

He walked into the small living room without turning on the lights. Leaning against the windowsill, he looked through the security bars out onto the city street below. A light spring rain fell and cast a shine over the asphalt. It brought to mind another time, another light rain, and the woman who had been in his arms.

Amanda. A pain pierced straight through him. Sweetness, light, meaning. He remembered getting up in the morning in Branchport and looking forward to the day ahead. Sometime, somehow, he would see her, if only a glimpse as he passed through the municipal center to the station. He closed his eyes and conjured up the feeling of anticipation that had surged through him each and every time he saw her. He recalled the drive up to the Catskills for their weekend away and her surprise when the resort had come into view. He remembered the smell of her hair, the taste of her mouth, the feel of her hands on his body. But most of all, he remembered the look on her face when they made love.

Some people across the street caught his attention as they left the all-night deli, joking and laughing loudly as they stumbled down the street. A homeless man lay on a subway grating not far from the entrance, and the people climbed over him, never looking down at the person under the cardboard boxes.

People here care about one another and help one another, not like the city where they step over bodies in the street....

Amanda's words came back to him with crystal clarity as he watched the group disappear from view. He had been too busy being condescending to small-town life to really understand what she had been saying then, but he did now.

Peace. He'd said that to her when she'd asked him why he'd taken on the job of sheriff of Branchport. He remembered the absolute quiet of that first night in the cabin on the lake. He'd hardly slept at all that night because it had been so damned quiet. And now he couldn't sleep for all the noise. The nightmares about

Ed's death had been frequent and intense back then, and now they were gone, replaced by a small, gamine face framed with brown curls and erotic fantasies he had no business indulging in.

Funny, he thought how one town, one woman could change his perspective on things. He wondered if Amanda slept well these nights since he'd left. He'd called her, of course, and she'd been friendly but there was that underlying coolness she couldn't or wouldn't hide. She barely managed to make small talk with him—she'd finally bought a new car; Kim and Tommy were kind of "going steady;" and Sean liked the new karate instructor.

She was distancing herself from him, and he didn't like it one bit. During his last call he had asked questions and received those cute one-word answers of hers in return until the telephone had become as heavy in his hand as the awkwardness in his voice. What did he expect? She had a home to run, kids to raise, and he was hundreds of miles away trying to decide what next to do with his life.

More and more the thought of returning to Branchport tempted him. He knew why he wanted to go back; he needed Amanda in his life. How? was the loaded question. He had no job and no source of income other than his pension. Somehow he didn't see himself as a clerk in John's hardware store. He was a cop, but working as a deputy under Odus with Sam Halverson was unappealing even if they did need the help, which they didn't. He wasn't about to plop himself down on Amanda's doorstep with no prospects and no plan.

The thought sat like a five hundred pound elephant on his gut as he strode away from the window and flopped back down onto his bed. He yawned loudly, scratched his day-old stubble and closed his eyes, trying to clear his mind of all thought so that sleep could claim him.

He'd almost succeeded when a sanitation truck's brakes screeched to a halt in front of his building. The metal cans banged against the metal of the truck as the men emptied the garbage. Vince groaned. He threw his forearm across his eyes and thanked heaven for small favors. At least the people next door had stopped fighting.

He must have dozed off sometime during the night because the next thing he knew, the rain had stopped and sunshine poured through his bedroom window. He opened his eyes, lifted his head and blinked away the remnants of sleep until he realized what woke him. The phone was ringing incessantly. He reached over and picked up the receiver, cradling it between his shoulder and neck as he plopped his head back down on the pillow.

"Hello?" he croaked.

"Vince? Mike Powell. Sorry to call so early, but I needed to talk to you. Got a minute?"

She hadn't realized it would hurt so much, physically hurt. Amanda filled the dishwasher with the dirty breakfast dishes. The kids had left for school, and she was alone in the house. Unconsciously she massaged a spot on her stomach where the knot had taken up permanent residence. Since Vince had left, this feeling of total desolation would, at odd moments such as this, crash over her like a tidal wave of despair. Taking two deep breaths, she leaned against the kitchen counter.

There was no earthly reason for her to feel this way. She'd known from the very beginning that Vince wasn't here to stay. So why was this lead weight pressing on her? Why couldn't she breathe in and out without herculean effort? And why was her throat constantly clogged with unshed tears?

Her head swam in a sea of uncharted emotion, and she wasn't able to think coherently. Since he'd gone, she'd been hiding. Hiding in her home, her work, her children.

Vince had kept in touch, just as he'd said he would, but she always found an excuse to cut the call short. What was the point? Prolonged, sad goodbyes would do neither of them any good, and she wanted no part of them. He was back home now, and she had to get on with her life.

Never before had her routine been so important. She disciplined herself to get up each morning, go to work, cook, clean, handle the children—all the while aiming for that time of day when she could drop into bed exhausted and cease to think at all.

She could handle it, she told herself as she finished cleaning up the kitchen table. She could even handle the looks of pity from the townspeople as she met them on the street. She'd been through this before, and it would pass. Time would heal all, and she was strong; she knew that from experience.

Amanda checked herself in the hallway mirror before leaving for work. She looked very professional in her navy-blue suit and white blouse, as if she hadn't a care in the world. How deceiving looks can be, she thought as she climbed into her brand-new red Honda and started the engine. She'd bought the car two weeks ago, and every time she sat in it, she was reminded of Vince and the day they'd spent together in the Catskills.

It was funny how suddenly *everything* reminded her of him. She found herself looking up from her desk several times during the day, expecting to see him standing there framed in the doorway, dropping in for a quick visit. Walking down the street, she would stop dead when a patrol car passed by, forcing herself not to peek inside, knowing he wouldn't—couldn't—be there. And every time Tommy came bounding into the house with a smile on his face, she was reminded of Vince and how he'd helped the boy.

In the short time he'd been in Branchport, he'd made an indelible mark. In some ways the town seemed more his than hers now. Strangely, that didn't bother her. She just wished he were here to share it. But she'd made herself a promise not to beg him to come back. He had to want the town as much as he wanted her.

But wishing did no good. Miracles didn't happen. She parked the car and walked into the municipal center. Mike was sitting at her desk scribbling a note on her pad.

"Good morning," she said.

"Amanda!" Mike looked up. "Good morning. I was just leaving you a note. I have to go out for about an hour, but I'll be back in time for the town council meeting at eleven."

"I didn't know we had a town council meeting scheduled for this morning," she said. "I saw John yesterday, and he didn't mention it."

"It wasn't scheduled. I called everyone early this morning. Kind of impromptu. I'll need you to sit in," he said as he crumpled the note in his hand and threw the balled paper in the wastebasket.

"No problem. Do you want me to take notes?"

Mike grinned. "That's a great idea!"

Amanda returned a wry smile, puzzled by his unusually exuberant mood. "Sure thing, Mike."

She shook her head as he waved her off and practically skipped out of the office. Strange, she thought, then shrugged, and sat down to get to work.

The various members of the town council, including her brother, John, ambled in to the conference room at the assigned time.

"What's this all about?" John asked her as he took the seat next to her.

"I really don't know."

"Must be pretty important. He called and woke me up at the crack of dawn."

"Well, I guess we'll soon find out. Here comes Mike now."

The eight town-council members and Amanda settled back in their seats as Mike formally opened the meeting. Amanda flipped through her pad to jot down notes she thought pertinent. Every time she glanced up at Mike, he grinned at her, or winked at her, as if they shared a secret. He reminded her of Sean in the way he was acting—a little boy with a big secret he couldn't wait to tell. What *was* he up to?

"And now to get to the real purpose of this meeting," Mike said, and extracted a letter from his folder. "It is with great regret that I accepted the resignation of one of the finest men I've ever known. Not only has Odus Tucker been sheriff of Branchport for thirty-five years, he's been a friend and father figure to each and every one of us in the room...."

Amanda's mind went blank as Mike continued to wax poetic on the attributes and career of Odus. A tingling feeling of anticipation ran up her back, and she shook it off. She tried to catch Mike's eye, but he now avoided her. She looked to John, but his attention was riveted on Mike.

"...So, as you can see, I had to accept the resignation. Odus realized that his health can no longer endure the rigors of the job. His age and the heart attack took more out of him than he thought. This is his decision, and I recommend that we vote to accept it."

"What do we do now, Mike?" one of the councilmen asked. "Who's going to replace Odus?"

"Well, I thought we might promote Sam Halverson—"

"You've got to be kidding," John said. "Sam's a great guy, but he's no manager. The other officers walk all over him as it is. Can you see the state of the department with him at its head?"

"I agree completely," Mike said. "So I took it upon myself to come up with an alternate candidate."

Once again, Mike favored Amanda with a grin. She sat up straighter in her chair as he turned from the group and headed for the conference room door. The blood drained from her face as the door swung open and Mike poked his head outside. No, no, no, her head repeated; but her heart was thumping triple time—yes, yes, yes. Muttered words were spoken, and then, suddenly—simply—he was there.

Vince stepped into the room, and a simultaneous cheer went up as each man present rose to his feet to greet him. She watched him smile and return the handshakes as he expressed his gratitude for their warm friendship and the chorus of "welcome backs."

Vince didn't look at her, didn't even glance her way. He couldn't. If he looked at her now, he'd never pull this off. He'd run over to her and pick her up and carry her out of this room to make love to her who knew where. He had it *that* bad. His body had been teetering on the threshold of arousal from the minute he'd hung up the phone with Mike. The ride up from the city had been interminable. Knowing it would only be a matter of hours until he saw her was almost too much to bear after all this time away. He felt her stare of disbelief, and allowed himself the pleasure of her reaction to his unexpected return.

She looked beautiful to his starved eyes. The blue suit and white blouse reminded him of a prim girls' school uniform. His imagination was running wild with thoughts of peeling it off of her, layer by layer until his hands reached her creamy skin. As he shook each man's hand, all he could think about was being alone and naked in bed with her.

Amanda sat stone-still, her hands icy, her throat closed. As hundreds of thoughts skipped through her mind, only one registered. *He's here. He's come back to the town. To me.*

"I suppose we should make a formal motion and officially vote Vince back as sheriff of Branchport," Mike said.

As the members were individually polled, Vince moved from the head of the table toward her end. He stood across from her, and, finally, their eyes met. He wasn't smiling anymore. Those gray penetrating eyes caressed her face. She wanted to reach out to him, touch each feature, feel his pulsing life beneath her fingers, prove to herself he was really here and not just a much-desired figment of her imagination.

"It's unanimous!" Mike announced.

Vince placed his palms midway across the conference table and leaned forward, his face only inches away from Amanda's.

"Not quite," he said. "Mrs. Simpson hasn't voted."

Amanda licked her lips as the heat coiled inside rose to the surface to stain her face with a soft, pink blush. "I'm not on the council," she said with a shaky voice, all too aware that every eye in the room was on her. "My vote doesn't count."

Vince shook his head back and forth, slowly, methodically. "Ah, but that's where you're wrong, Amanda," he said. "Your vote is the only one that *does* count." He brushed his lips against hers, oblivious to the intent stares of the men in the room. "What do you say? Am I the best man for the job?"

Amanda brought her hands up to his face and rubbed her palms against the freshly shaven skin on his cheeks. "Oh, yes, Sheriff," she whispered, her heart filled with love. "You're the best man, period."

She tilted her head and leaned into his kiss. Unselfconsciously his tongue entered her mouth and delved deep inside as he kissed her with a love and a hunger that could no longer be hidden or denied.

Amanda heard a background cheer go up, and dimly acknowledged the approval of their audience. She was vaguely aware that the meeting ended and the council dispersed, discreetly leaving them alone in the room. Vince lifted his mouth from hers, and the way he looked at her caused her eyes to mist.

"I love you," he said softly, irrevocably.

"And I love you."

"I wish I could show you how much right now, but I can't. I have to go over to the station for a while. I'll be back as soon as I can."

She nodded and reluctantly let him go. Slowly she returned to her office in a daze and sat down, not quite able to take in all that had just happened. But two facts were blatantly clear. He was back, and he loved her. To her mind, nothing else mattered.

"Why do I get the feeling you'll be good for nothing today, Amanda?"

She looked up at Mike's face.

"Why didn't you tell me?"

"And spoil the surprise?" He laughed. "Go home, Amanda. Take the rest of the day off. It's only noon, and in your state of mind, you're not going to accomplish anything here. I'll tell Vince you left early if he comes back."

She didn't need to be told twice. Amanda left and went straight home, excited as a child on Christmas morning. She knew exactly what she was going to do. Once upstairs, she stripped the white cotton sheets off her bed and replaced them with the brand new beige satin ones she'd bought.

Nervously she rummaged through her drawers until she came up with what she was looking for. She held the negligee up to her image in the mirror and smiled. The pale blue nightgown was decorated with strategically placed embroidered lace up one side, revealing just a glimpse of what laid beneath. Perfect. Quickly and efficiently, she changed from her proper business suit into the sheer nightgown. She was about to put a brush to her curls when the doorbell rang.

Rubbing her damp palms together, she inhaled deeply and trotted down the stairs in bare feet. She opened the front door, and, like the first time she met him, came face-to-face with the shiny tin Sheriff star; but this time, as her eyes traveled from the badge to the face of the owner, there was no stern, serious expression. What she saw now chilled her more than that long-forgotten blast of January air. What she saw now was love, and a very obvious, barely constrained look of desire.

"Amanda? What are you wearing? My God—"

"Come in, Sheriff," she said coyly, pulling him by the hand into the hallway. Slamming the door firmly shut, she rested her back against it and smiled at him.

Vince took one look at her and threw his hat across to the sofa. With one giant step, he was upon her, one arm on each side of her, pinning her to the door.

"Uh-uh," she said, and dipped out from under his arms to elude his grasp. She took hold of his hand and led him toward the stairs.

"What are you up to?" He grinned.

"Come on upstairs and find out," she taunted. "I have a welcome back gift for you."

Vince followed her up the stairs and into her bedroom. He noticed the turned-down bed and satin sheets immediately, and his already heated blood began to pump faster. Amanda came up to him and unbuttoned his shirt first before reaching down to his belt buckle. She took off the nightstick and cuffs and dropped them onto the chair. The holster and gun followed. Then her efficient fingers opened his pants. The grating sound of the zipper cut the air in the quiet room. Amanda gently eased her hand into the opening and caressed him.

"Oh, sweetheart . . ."

His deep, low moan gratified her ears, but she wasn't through yet. Not by a long shot.

She led him to the bed and lay down in a seductive pose across the glossy sheets. Her eyes never leaving his, she patted the spot next to her for him to join her. The weight of the mattress dipped as Vince kneeled over her. His eyes were fierce and alive with hunger, his jaw taut with desire, his mouth full and sensuous, ready to devour her whole.

"I've been having some very erotic dreams about you this past month," he said.

"As I have about you," she whispered and reached up to pull him down to her. "I'll act out mine, if you'll act out yours."

Vince smiled, a slow, sexy, promising smile. "Come here."

She did. Their lips met with a strong, urgent need to get as close as possible. His tongue dipped into her mouth and caressed the recesses within, mimicking the act of love. The feel and taste of him were the nourishment her parched body craved, and she drank greedily.

Within minutes their clothes were gone, and they rolled around the bed allowing the slippery sheets to simultaneously cool and arouse their fevered senses. Vince kissed her neck, her ear, and left a trail of kisses en route to the final destination of her breasts. He licked one tight bud, then the other, before taking her into his mouth and suckling each in turn.

Amanda writhed against the onslaught of sensations that were spinning her out of control. She'd loved making love with him before, but now, today, knowing he was here to stay, knowing that he loved her, the feelings were gloriously magnified. She ran her hands over his body and caressed him intimately.

Vince lifted his head and stared into her eyes. He wanted this moment to last forever, but he was fast losing control of his body's responses. There were so many things he wanted to do to her, with her, but an urgency gripped him and he was lost. He had to have her, be inside of her, together with her in body as completely and fully as he was in his mind and heart. And God help him, but he couldn't wait any longer.

He poised his body over hers and kissed her as he slowly, carefully, inch-by-inch joined himself to her in a rhapsody of love.

"I love you, Amanda Simpson," he said in a harsh, barely controlled whisper. "More than I ever thought it possible to love."

Amanda arched her back and reveled in the feeling of fullness. "Show me."

He gave her all he had to give as they moved together in a rhythm as old and sacred as time itself; each certain and secure in the knowledge that no two people, ever, had loved this deeply or profoundly.

When the bright lights of fulfillment flashed within her, Amanda called out his name in a prayerful chant. Vince fought a losing battle within himself to control his own action, but it was too late. Her uninhibited response pulled him over the edge. He entwined the fingers of both hands with hers and raised her arms above her head as he joined her in the total and absolute expression of their love.

He cradled her body to his as they floated back to reality. Amanda studied his face as she traced a finger over his brow. He looked thinner to her starved eyes, but there was also an inner calmness radiating out of him. The cloudy look was gone; he seemed at peace with himself.

"Is it my imagination," she said as she caressed his cheek, "or has something changed?"

He took hold of her hand and kissed the palm, a half smile on his face. "Am I that transparent?"

"To me you are. What's happened?"

Vince's gaze locked with hers. "I went to see the mother of the boy I killed."

"And?"

"And we talked. About everything. I came away feeling better than I had in years."

"You've forgiven yourself," she said softly.

He nodded slightly. "Yes, I think I have. You were right, you know. It won't ever go away completely. But I can live with it now. I can go on from here." He brushed his lips against her fingertips.

"I'm happy for you. And for us."

She moved her hand from his lips and kissed him. As he deepened the kiss she knew it was his silent way of showing his gratitude to her for her understanding and support. She felt her body stir as he pulled her to lay on top of him.

"We should get married."

Amanda looked down at him, an amused expression on her face. "Is that a proposal, Sheriff? Or an order?"

He tweaked her nose. "A proposal. Not a very good one, come to think of it. But my heart is in the right place."

Amanda ran her hands over him. "That's not all."

He grabbed her roaming hands to still them.

"Will you marry me?" he asked seriously.

"Yes," she said. "Anytime, anywhere, anyhow."

He kissed her lips gently, softly, sealing their promise.

"Whew!" he said. "That's a relief. I heard the owners rented out the cabin for the summer. If you'd have said no, I'd have no place to live!"

"Why you . . ."

Vince laughed and jumped from the bed to escape her playful attack. He slipped into his underwear and walked over toward the bedroom window to look outside. Suddenly he jumped back.

"Uh-oh. Hester Waterbury is in the driveway looking over the squad car."

Amanda got up from the bed and grabbed the top sheet to wrap around her body. She walked up to the window, but Vince put out an arm to stop her.

"She'll see you," he warned.

Amanda brushed his arm away and walked right up to the window, pulling the curtain aside to peer out at

Hester. Vince came up behind her and put an arm around her shoulder. Just then, Hester Waterbury looked up. For a moment the old woman just stared at the two of them, mouth opened in disbelief at what she saw.

Amanda waved down to her, a huge smile on her face. "Just think, Hester," she said out loud, even though the old woman couldn't hear her. "In broad daylight! What is the world coming to?"

Vince hugged her to him and gave her a quick kiss on the lips. The next time they looked down, they both laughed at the sight of Hester scurrying across the street like a squirrel with a hoard of the finest acorns.

Vince turned Amanda to face him. "You realize that by dinnertime tonight the good people of Branchport will be talking about this."

Amanda drew herself up onto her tiptoes and brushed her lips against his. "Let them talk...."

*   *   *   *   *

Take 4 bestselling love stories FREE

Plus get a FREE surprise gift!

PASSPORT TO ROMANCE
SWEEPSTAKES RULES

1 **HOW TO ENTER:** To enter, you must be the age of majority and complete the official entry form, or print your name, address, telephone number and age on a plain piece of paper and mail to: Passport to Romance, P.O. Box 9056, Buffalo, NY 14269-9056. No mechanically reproduced entries accepted.

2 All entries must be received by the CONTEST CLOSING DATE, DECEMBER 31, 1990 TO BE ELIGIBLE.

3. **THE PRIZES:** There will be ten (10) Grand Prizes awarded, each consisting of a choice of a trip for two people from the following list:
   i)   London, England (approximate retail value $5,050 U.S.)
   ii)   England, Wales and Scotland (approximate retail value $6,400 U.S.)
   iii) Carribean Cruise (approximate retail value $7,300 U.S.)
   iv)   Hawaii (approximate retail value $9,550 U.S.)
   v)   Greek Island Cruise in the Mediterranean (approximate retail value $12,250 U.S.)
   vi)   France (approximate retail value $7,300 U.S.)

4 Any winner may choose to receive any trip or a cash alternative prize of $5,000.00 U.S. in lieu of the trip.

5. **GENERAL RULES:** Odds of winning depend on number of entries received.

6. A random draw will be made by Nielsen Promotion Services, an independent judging organization, on January 29, 1991, in Buffalo, NY, at 11:30 a.m from all eligible entries received on or before the Contest Closing Date

7 Any Canadian entrants who are selected must correctly answer a time-limited mathematical skill-testing question in order to win

8 Full contest rules may be obtained by sending a stamped, self-addressed envelope to "Passport to Romance Rules Request", P.O. Box 9998, Saint John, New Brunswick, Canada E2L 4N4.

9 Quebec residents may submit any litigation respecting the conduct and awarding of a prize in this contest to the Régie des loteries et courses du Québec

10. Payment of taxes other than air and hotel taxes is the sole responsibility of the winner

11 Void where prohibited by law

COUPON BOOKLET OFFER TERMS

To receive your Free travel-savings coupon booklets, complete the mail-in Offer Certificate on the preceeding page, including the necessary number of proofs-of-purchase, and mail to: Passport to Romance, P.O. Box 9057, Buffalo, NY 14269-9057. The coupon booklets include savings on travel-related products such as car rentals, hotels, cruises, flowers and restaurants. Some restrictions apply. The offer is available in the United States and Canada. Requests must be postmarked by January 25, 1991. Only proofs-of-purchase from specially marked "Passport to Romance" Harlequin® or Silhouette® books will be accepted. The offer certificate must accompany your request and may not be reproduced in any manner. Offer void where prohibited or restricted by law. LIMIT FOUR COUPON BOOKLETS PER NAME, FAMILY, GROUP, ORGANIZATION OR ADDRESS. Please allow up to 8 weeks after receipt of order for shipment. Enter quickly as quantities are limited. Unfulfilled mail-in offer requests will receive free Harlequin® or Silhouette® books (not previously available in retail stores), in quantities equal to the number of proofs-of-purchase required for Levels One to Four, as applicable.

PR-SWPS

OFFICIAL SWEEPSTAKES ENTRY FORM

Complete and return this Entry Form immediately—the more Entry Forms you submit, the better your chances of winning!
- Entry Forms must be received by **December 31, 1990**
- A random draw will take place on **January 29, 1991**
- Trip must be taken by **December 31, 1991**

3-SD-1-SW

YES, I want to win a PASSPORT TO ROMANCE vacation for two! I understand the prize includes round-trip air fare, accommodation and a daily spending allowance.

Name_____

Address_____

City_____ State_____ Zip_____

Telephone Number_____ Age_____

Return entries to: **PASSPORT TO ROMANCE**, P.O. Box 9056, Buffalo, NY 14269-9056

COUPON BOOKLET/OFFER CERTIFICATE

Item	LEVEL ONE Booklet 1	LEVEL TWO Booklet 1 & 2	LEVEL THREE Booklet 1, 2 & 3	LEVEL FOUR Booklet 1, 2, 3 & 4
Booklet 1 = $100+	$100+	$100+	$100+	$100+
Booklet 2 = $200+		$200+	$200+	$200+
Booklet 3 = $300+			$300+	$300+
Booklet 4 = $400+	____	____	____	$400+
Approximate Total Value of Savings	$100+	$300+	$600+	$1,000+
# of Proofs of Purchase Required	4	6	12	18
Check One	____	____	____	____

Name_____

Address_____

City_____ State_____ Zip_____

Return Offer Certificates to: **PASSPORT TO ROMANCE**, P.O. Box 9057, Buffalo, NY 14269-9057

Requests must be postmarked by **January 25, 1991**

- ✂ - - - -

 ONE PROOF OF PURCHASE

3-SD-1

To collect your free coupon booklet you must include the necessary number of proofs-of-purchase with a properly completed Offer Certificate

See previous page for details